DOCTOR WHO AND
THE IMAGE OF THE FENDAHL

DOCTOR WHO AND THE IMAGE OF THE FENDAHL

Based on the BBC television serial by Chris Boucher by arrangement with the British Broadcasting Corporation

TERRANCE DICKS

A TARGET BOOK
published by
the Paperback Division of
W. H. ALLEN & CO. LTD

A Target Book
Published in 1979
by the Paperback Division of W.H. Allen & Co. Ltd
A Howard & Wyndham Company
44 Hill Street, London W1X 8LB

Reprinted 1979
Reprinted 1980
Reprinted 1982

Printed and bound in Great Britain by
Cox & Wyman Ltd, Reading

ISBN 0 426 20077 2

Contents

1

The Skull

A man was hurrying through the woods. Dusk was falling, and the road was dark and lonely. Wakening owls hooted mournfully in the shadowy tree-tops. The hiker was near the end of his day's travel. He thought longingly of the crowded bar of some village pub, of pints of beer and cheese rolls, of lights and tobacco smoke and the babble of conversation.

He kept thinking someone was following him.

It was ridiculous, of course. Every time he looked over his shoulder the lane behind him was quite empty. But somehow the sensation persisted. He could feel something, some presence, some threat, looming up behind him. An old verse began running through his head. How did it go?

> 'Like one that walks a lonely road
> And dares not turn his head
> Because he knows a frightful fiend
> Doth close behind him tread ...'

Something like that, anyway. 'A frightful fiend...' Trying to put the rhyme out of his mind, the walker hurried on his way.

Professor Adam Colby glared at the skull.

The skull, despite its blankly shadowed eye-sockets, seemed to glare right back at him.

Colby sighed. He was a handsome, rather elegant young man, neat and cat-like, whose languid manner concealed a brilliant brain. 'Well, don't just sit there, Eustace. Say something.'

The skull, of course, said nothing. Enthroned on its gleaming metal stand, it dominated the clutter of chemical flasks, bunsen burners, slide rules, callipers and clip-boards that surrounded it.

Colby scowled. The skull represented a triumph, a challenge and an enigma, and his laboured student joke of christening it Eustace did nothing to relieve the problem.

The skull was an impossibility.

Not that you could tell by looking at it. A human skull, well-developed brain-case, obviously of great antiquity. Fine cracks and hair-lines across the yellowing bone of its surface showed that it had been painstakingly reconstructed from various different-sized fragments.

Colby sighed theatrically, attracting the attention of the young woman peering through a microscope at the nearby workbench. She was in her late twenties, dark-haired, and even in a plain white lab coat and slacks, strikingly attractive. Her name was Thea Ransome. In her own way she was almost as distinguished a scientist as Colby himself.

She looked at Colby and smiled. 'Why don't you just publish? Announce your discovery of Eustace to the world and be done with it?'

'Why should anyone believe me?' asked Colby plaintively. 'I found him—and I don't!'

'Are you questioning my technical competence?'

'Of course not. The volcanic sediment in which the skull was embedded was twelve million years

8

old.' Colby gave her a mock bow. 'I accept without reservation the results of your excellent potassium-argon test. What I don't accept is that Eustace here managed to get himself buried under a volcano at least eight million years before he could have existed!'

Thea shrugged. Her job was the dating of the most ancient objects by the most advanced scientific methods. Fitting the results into the accepted theories was someone else's problem.

The lab door was flung open and Max Stael appeared, looking round the untidy laboratory with distaste, like a Prussian Officer on the parade ground. His stiff Germanic good looks reflected his stiff Germanic character. His lab coat was crisp and gleaming white. 'Professor Colby, Doctor Fendleman is waiting for the corrected co-ordinates.'

Lazily Colby stretched out his arm, fished a clipboard from the cluttered bench and held it out. 'There you go.'

Stael took the clip-board, tucked it under his arm, gave a brisk nod, and turned to leave.

'Come on, Maxie,' said Colby encouragingly. 'End the day with a smile.'

Max Stael stared blankly at him for a moment. Then his rather woodenly handsome features twitched briefly, and he turned and left the laboratory.

Colby winked at Thea, rose and stretched. 'Think I'll call it a day. Coming, Thea?'

'I just want to finish this—shan't be long.'

Colby gave a farewell nod to the skull and drifted off. Thea returned to her microscope.

It was almost dark now and the walker increased his pace, looking uneasily around at the gathering shadows. He began to whistle to keep up his spirits, a ragged uneven version of some ragtime tune. The owls seemed to accompany him with a mocking, hooted chorus.

His sense of oppression, the feeling of being somehow pursued was stronger than ever now. The night-wind rustled eerily through the trees as he hurried on.

Stael went along an oak-panelled corridor in the rear wing of Fetch Priory. The atmosphere was cold and dank, as if this part of the enormous old building was seldom used. He marched up to a heavy oak door, produced a formidable-looking set of keys, unlocked the door and went into the room beyond.

The big old-fashioned room had been converted into an incredibly complex electronic laboratory, its walls lined with banks of controls. This was the home of the Time Scanner, Doctor Fendleman's supreme achievement, and as yet a closely-guarded secret from all but one of his colleagues. The apparatus gave out a steady electronic tick.

The left-hand bank controlled and monitored power input, the right directional co-ordinates. The huge central bank running across the entire rear wall was the control console for the Time Displacement Sweep. There was a large vision-screen at its centre, a number of smaller monitor-screens at each side.

Fendleman was busy with the computer controls, a wiry intense-looking man, sharp-faced, with a thin moustache. Nothing particularly impressive about him—but he was one of the richest and most powerful men in the world. Fendleman Electronics was a multi-national giant that had outstripped all its competitors, an industrial complex so vast that it virtually ran itself—leaving Fendleman free to pursue his twin hobbies of archaeology and electronic research.

He looked up as Stael came into the room. 'Ah, good, there you are Max.' Stael handed him the co-ordinates, and he studied them for a moment. 'Yes, excellent. We are ready to begin. Phase one power please.'

Stael moved to the power console. 'Phase one power.' A steadily rising electronic hum filled the cellar.

'Phase two power.'

'Phase two power,' said Stael obediently. The hum became a high-pitched, vibrating whine. Stael winced, rubbed a hand over his eyes, shook his head as if to clear it, and then returned his attention to the console.

Alone in the laboratory on the floor above, Thea Ransome winced, and rubbed her forehead. Her eyes fell on the skull, and were held by it. There was something very strange about the skull. It seemed to be *glowing* . . . She moved over to take a closer look

'Switching to main computer control,' said Fendleman. There was a chattering beep of computer sound, which just as suddenly cut out.

11

'Activating full power run-up sequence—now!'

The whine of power rose higher. The lights in the cellar flickered and dimmed.

The lights in Professor Colby's laboratory dimmed too. For a moment Thea glanced up at them. Then she returned to her absorbed study of the skull.

It was quite definitely glowing now, and as the glow became brighter, all expression and vitality faded from Thea's features. It was as though the skull were absorbing her very being. Her face became blank, her eyes glazed, like a high priestess enraptured by some ancient ritual . . . She seemed to absorb the skull and yet to become part of it . . .

Worried by the ever-approaching darkness, the hiker stopped, fished a heavy torch from his rucksack and waved it around. The white beam picked out trees and bushes, nothing else. Yet somehow the hiker *knew* there was something hunting him. He began to run, blundering from the path, crashing panic-stricken through the bushes.

From somewhere close behind him there came a strange, slurred dragging sound, as *something* slithered after him . . . He stumbled on blindly. Then suddenly his legs refused to obey him. 'I can't move . . .' he babbled. *'I can't move my legs . . .'*

The dragging sound came closer.

Thea Ransome could see nothing, feel nothing but the skull, as its glow rose to a fierce intensity. The

12

power-hum of Fendleman's equipment had pene-
trated the laboratory now, and in Thea's mind
another sound mingled with it. A slurred dragging
sound . . .

The hiker stared upwards in helpless fascination.
There was a hissing, hungry sound as the thing
swooped down. He fell back, dropping his torch, and
gave one last terrible death-cry as the life-force was
sucked out of him.

The hiker's dying scream echoed through Thea
Ransome's mind. The glow of the skull faded, and
she fainted, falling from the stool.

In Fendleman's laboratory the electronic scream rose
a notch higher and then steadied. 'Running at full
power, Doctor Fendleman.'
    'Excellent. We can begin the Time Scan.' Fendle-
man's long white hands moved over the controls.
'Commencing scan. Programme one . . .'

Somewhere in the Space Time continuum there was a
police box that was not a police box at all. Inside its
impossibly-large control room, a tall, casually
dressed man with bright blue eyes and a crop of curly
hair was studying the electronic innards of what
appeared to be some kind of robot dog. A dark-
haired girl in a brief animal-skin costume looked on
disapprovingly. 'Professor Marius will not be
pleased.'

13

The robot dog was called K9. In reality a mobile self-powered computer with defensive capabilities, K9 had been presented to the Doctor by his creator and first owner, Professor Marius. The automaton had developed some mysterious ailment, and the Doctor was trying to assess the damage. 'Nasty,' he muttered, shaking his head. 'Very nasty.'

'Will he be all right?' asked Leela anxiously. She was fond of K9.

'Ssh! I don't know yet.' The Doctor concluded his examination. '*It* will be perfectly all right. *It* just has a little corrosion in its circuits.'

'I can call K9 "he" if I want to! After all, you call the TARDIS "she".'

'Never!'

'Yes you do, I've heard you—you called it she just a moment ago.'

Ignoring her the Doctor went on with his examination.

'And another thing. It is quite clear to me that you cannot really control this old machine.'

The Doctor was shocked. 'What did you say, Leela? No, I heard what you said!'

'Then why ask?'

'Leela, I understand the TARDIS perfectly. There's not a single part of her that I haven't adjusted or repaired at some time or another.'

'Well, don't cry about it!' said Leela mockingly.

The Doctor stood up. 'What is more,' he said with dignity, 'I am in complete and constant control of her——'

The soothing hum coming from the console changed to a high-pitched note of distress, and the TARDIS gave a sudden lurch.

14

Leela grabbed the edge of the console. 'What's happening?'

The Doctor was studying dials on the console. 'We seem to be being dragged towards a Relative Continuum Displacement Zone.'

'A what?'

'A hole in Time!'

'What's going to happen to us?'

'I wish I knew!' yelled the Doctor. 'I just wish I knew. We're completely out of control!'

2

Dead Man in the Wood

The TARDIS seemed to be spinning and twisting and falling all at the same time as if caught in some temporal whirlpool.

Leela clung desperately to the console. 'Can we break free, Doctor?'

The Doctor was clawing his way round the console, stabbing frantically at the controls. 'I don't know. It all depends on this misunderstood, uncontrollable *old* machine of mine.'

Leela bowed to the juddering centre column of the TARDIS, as if to some powerful idol. 'I'm sorry—I meant no disrespect!'

Slowly the sickening spinning began to lessen. 'She's turning!' shouted the Doctor. 'We're coming out of it!'

Encouraged by the success of her prayer, Leela bowed again. 'Forgive me, I was wrong to be disrespectful.'

The TARDIS steadied herself still more, and quite suddenly things were back to normal. The Doctor laughed exultantly, and patted the console. 'TARDIS, you are *wonderful*!'

The console gave a pleased electronic burble. Leela stared at it in awe. 'You didn't tell me! Can she really understand every word we say?'

'Well, yes in a way. She generates a low-intensity telepathic field. Obviously your primitive thought patterns appeal to her.'

Leela wasn't sure if this was a compliment or not. 'They do?'

'Yes, you see——' the Doctor broke off. 'That's odd.'

'What is, my thought patterns?'

'The turbulence must have upset the instruments. I can't get any proper readings.'

'What does that mean?'

'It means I can't calculate our co-ordinates! We'll just have to follow the Time Scanner back to its source.'

'To destroy it?' suggested Leela eagerly. She wasn't even sure what a Time Scanner was, but it had obviously put them in some danger. Leela was a great believer in paying off old scores.

'We'll certainly have to stop it being used,' said the Doctor thoughtfully. 'If we don't it will cause a direct continuum implosion.'

'What will that do?'

'Destroy the planet it's operating from!'

'Do we know which one it is yet?'

The Doctor was brooding over the controls. 'That's what I'm trying to find out. It's partly guesswork, of course, but if my estimations are correct—oh no!'

'What is it?'

'Not that one!'

'Not what one?'

'Not there!'

Leela was jumping up and down with impatience. 'Not where?' she shrieked.

'Earth!' said the Doctor, with gloomy relish.

Leela couldn't understand why the Doctor was so

17

upset. She'd always believed Earth was one of his favourite planets. Perhaps the attraction had worn off when he'd been exiled there by the Time Lords. But he'd still liked it enough to take her to visit a Victorian Music Hall. Leela shuddered, remembering what that had led to . . .

The Doctor was looking severely at her. 'Your ancestors, Leela, have a talent for self destruction which is little short of genius.'

Leela's temper flared up. 'Now listen, Doctor, I do not like the way you keep talking about *my* ancestors . . .'

The Doctor grinned. 'I like your outfit.'

Baffled but pleased, Leela said, 'Thank you.'

'It's a pleasure,' said the Doctor politely, and went back to his calculations.

Leela felt she'd been outsmarted—but she couldn't quite work out how . . .

The kitchen of Fetch Priory was a large stone-flagged room which seemed to dwarf the newly-installed modern sink and cooker. It was a room which demanded an immense cast-iron cooking-range shining with blacklead, rows of gleaming copper pots and pans, and the legions of cooks and maids it took to run such a place, and make life comfortable for the gentry upstairs.

But there were no resident servants at the Priory these days, just a local cook who came in to prepare the evening meal. Fendleman could have afforded all the servants he wanted. But when he had taken the place over for his Research Centre, Fendleman had decided that living-in servants, who might gossip or even be bribed by some spying competitor, would be too great a risk. The scientists who worked at the Priory were paid the highest salaries in the field—but they had to make their own beds and cook some of their own meals all the same.

Thea Ransome was sitting at the big wooden table flicking through the paper, huddled over a mug of coffee she'd had to make herself. Fendleman and Max Stael came into the kitchen. They looked tired but triumphant.

'Ah, Thea,' said Fendleman vaguely. 'You're feeling all right again?'

Thea had recovered to find herself on the laboratory floor, late last evening. She had gone rather dazedly to bed, but had awakened next morning, feeling perfectly normal. 'Yes, I'm fine now, thanks. I still don't remember what happened. Must have spent too long peering into that microscope.' She stared with mock-severity at Stael. 'I do remember one thing though, Max. It was your turn to cook the breakfast!'

Stael returned her look with his usual impassivity. Thea sighed. There was no fun in teasing Max, he was totally without a sense of humour.

Fendleman said, 'I'm sorry, you must blame me for that. We have only just finished, we worked all night you know.' He rubbed his hands. 'And the results! I think the results will amaze even our sceptical friend Colby.' He looked round the kitchen 'Where is he by the way?'

Thea looked up from her paper. 'Out exercising Leakey.' Leakey was Adam Colby's dog, a scruffy old Labrador. His name was partly a tribute to the famous anthropologist, partly a reference to an unfortunate habit of occasionally forgetting his house-training.

At this precise moment Colby was not so much exercising Leakey as looking for him. Leakey loved to explore, and his first action when taken for a walk was to disappear in quest of some exciting smell. The rest of the walk was spent looking for him and persuading him to come back home.

Colby stood in the middle of the woods shouting patiently, 'Leakey! Come on Leakey, time to go home. Here, boy! Here!'

He heard a whine coming from a clump of bushes. 'Come on Leakey? What have you got boy? Found another bone?'

When he pushed his way through the bushes, Colby saw that Leakey had found not a bone but a body. A huddled shape lay face-down on the ground. Leakey was nosing around it, whining uneasily. Colby knelt to examine the body, feeling for a pulse in the neck. There was nothing. The man was clearly quite dead, and had been for some time. Curiously there was no sign of rigor mortis, the stiffening that comes after death. Instead, the body felt oddly soft and shapeless beneath his hands. Colby noticed something else—a strange mark on the back of the man's neck. He turned the body over, and recoiled.

The dead man's face was horribly twisted—eyes bulging in pure terror. Colby wondered what horror had put such a terrible look on the dead man's face.

Fendleman and Stael had finished breakfast by now, and were sitting over coffee in the kitchen.

Fendleman took a sip of coffee. 'Do not misunderstand me, Thea, I have the greatest respect for Adam Colby. His methodology cannot be faulted. The entire excavation was brilliant, and the reconstruction of the skull was first class work—I doubt if anyone else could have done it.'

Thea poured herself another cup of coffee. 'The evolutionary implications seem to worry him rather. He says he just can't accept them.'

Fendleman's eyes twinkled as if at some private joke. 'And you, Thea. Can you accept them?'

'Chronology is my field, Doctor Fendleman. I'm just a technician, not a palaeontologist.'

Colby burst into the kitchen, Leakey at his heels. 'There's a corpse at the edge of the wood!'

There was a brief, stunned silence. Fendleman rose slowly to his feet. 'What kind of a corpse?'

'A dead one of course,' said Colby impatiently. 'What other kind is there?'

'Is it male? Female?'

'Male.'

'Do we know him?' asked Thea.

Colby shook his head, still pale and shaken by the memory of what he had seen 'Well, I don't, never saw him before. On some kind of walking holiday by the look of him. Boots and a rucksack and all that . . .'

'How did he die?' asked Fendleman patiently, 'Are there any signs of violence?'

'Not exactly, though there was a mark on his neck . . .' Colby shook, remembering the dead man's face. 'But by the look of him—well, he didn't die easily.'

21

'It is never easy to die,' said Stael enigmatically.

'Well, thank you for that pearl of wisdom, Max,' said Colby satirically. 'I'm off to call the police.'

Fendleman's voice stopped him at the door. 'Just a moment, Adam. We must consider this very carefully.'

'What's to consider? There's a body out there. We can't just leave it—or are you breeding vultures in that secret laboratory of yours?'

This was an old grievance. Everyone knew Fendleman had some kind of electronics laboratory hidden away in the rear wing. So far he had refused to let anyone but Stael inside, or even to discuss the kind of work he was doing there—though he wasn't above dropping a variety of tantalising hints.

Fendleman took the taunt with dignified calm. 'Please, Adam! There is no need for discourtesy.'

Colby threw himself into a chair. 'Oh, I'm sorry. I suppose it must be shock.' His face clouded. 'He looked awful—absolutely awful—poor chap. He must have been utterly terrified when he died.'

'Now listen to me, Colby. You know that wood is supposed to be haunted? Can you imagine what would happen if there were news of a mysterious death?'

Colby stared blankly at him. It was Thea who realised the fear in Fendleman's mind. 'There'd be a certain amount of publicity, I suppose . . .'

'There would be a circus! That wood attracts enough local lunatics as it is, without advertising for more.'

There was a silence. Everyone knew that Fendleman was talking about Witchcraft and Black Magic. The village near the Priory was isolated and inbred, and there were strong rumours that the cult of the Old Ways still survived. Max Stael had even made a study of it—the occult was a hobby of his. He had discovered that Fetch Wood had always had an evil reputation. There were stories of mysterious ceremonies held in its groves at midnight, of chanting, cowled figures circling around secret altars . . . There was even a village witch—who also happened to be the Priory cook.

Colby said slowly, 'Even so, I don't see we've much alternative . . .'

Fendleman leaned across the table. 'Adam, our work here is at a critical stage. Your discovery of the skull is one of the most important milestones in human development. Your work will seriously affect the way man views himself. We cannot be interrupted at this moment of destiny.'

'Yes, but——'

Fendleman produced his strongest argument. 'And besides—we wouldn't want your Nobel prize to be jeopardised by an unfortunate coincidence. Now would we?'

Thea looked hard at him. 'Just what are you suggesting, Doctor Fendleman?'

'I am not suggesting anything, yet. When Adam has recovered he can show me the body, and we can decide what to do.' He paused. 'Perhaps we can arrange for the body to be discovered somewhere else.'

Thea was shocked. 'That's illegal!'

Fendleman shrugged. 'A harmless deception.'

She turned to Colby. 'Adam, you can't . . .'

Colby was looking thoughtful. For all his languid manner he was a fiercely ambitious man, and

Fendleman's remark about the Nobel prize had had its effect. 'It probably wouldn't make much difference, I suppose ... I mean the poor chap is dead now ...'

'Exactly,' said Fendleman heartily. 'Exactly! We'll work something out, eh Adam?' He ushered Colby out of the room, nodding to Stael to follow them.

Colby went on ahead and Fendleman took Stael to one side. 'Get on to London. Tell Hartman I want a Security Team here within two hours. Tell him I want the best men we have, and I want them armed.' Stael nodded and moved away. Fendleman stopped him. 'Oh, and one other thing. I want you to do a full post-mortem on that body. We've got to find out how that man died ...'

3

Time Scan

The centre column came slowly to rest, as the TARDIS landed. The Doctor touched a control, and the door swung open.

'Earth?' asked Leela cautiously.

'Earth!'

'The place of the Time Scan?'

'Yes—well, more or less. I haven't quite got it pin-pointed, but it's definitely round here—somewhere.'

Leela checked the knife at her belt. 'Come on then.'

The Doctor jammed his floppy hat on his head, and wound an incredibly long scarf round his neck. 'The one who leads says "Come on!" '

Leela stared at him.

'Come on!' said the Doctor, and strode from the TARDIS. With an exasperated sigh, Leela followed.

They found themselves in a field at the edge of a wood. It was a sunny summer morning and the TARDIS was surrounded by a herd of curious cows.

The Doctor raised his hat. 'Good morning! Which one of you ladies happens to be using a Time Scanner?'

The cows looked at him with large brown eyes. One of them mooed gently.

Leela gave the Doctor a sceptical look. 'This

doesn't seem like the right place for a Time Scanner, Doctor.'

'Well, I did say more or less.' The Doctor surveyed the peaceful rural scene. 'Though I must admit, this place does look rather less than more. You know, I really don't think these cows know anything about a Time Scanner.' He drew a deep breath. 'Still never mind, it's a beautiful day, and the exercise will do us good. Come on!'

He set off through the wood.

When Stael came into the laboratory, Fendleman was studying a computer print-out with absorbed attention. 'Look, it is all here, Stael, if only we can interpret it. If we can get a visual representation of this, then we will see the living owner of that skull!'

Stael glanced at the print-out. There were other things on his mind. 'I have completed the post mortem on the body found in the wood.'

'And?'

'I cannot find the cause of death. There is a small blister on the back of the neck, close to the base of the skull, but that could not have killed him.'

'Natural causes then?'

Stael shook his head. 'I do not think so. There is something—strange.'

'Well?'

Stael paused, collecting his thoughts. 'The outward signs are that the man died very recently. His watch is still working, he has yesterday's newspaper in his pocket, the coffee in the thermos in his pack was still hot, the mud on his boots——'

'Yes, yes,' interrupted Fendleman impatiently. 'Get on with it!'

'The body is decomposing.'

'Already?' Fendleman's voice was shocked.

'It's happening almost as you watch.'

'And the cause?'

'I don't know . . . It's as if all the energy has been removed. All the binding force is gone, and all that's left is a husk.'

Fendleman was silent for a moment, considering. He looked at Stael, the same thought in both their minds. The Time Scanner was a totally new piece of equipment, which produced disturbances in the fabric of Time itself. They had always known that there was a danger that its use might produce side effects. It seemed horribly likely that the death of the man in the wood was one of them.

'Very well,' said Fendleman decisively. 'Are the security team in place?'

'Yes.'

'Good. You will dispose of the body, Max. No one must know of this. No one at all.'

Stael nodded and went out of the laboratory. Fendleman sat staring into space for a moment. He was breaking the law, but that didn't matter; he was rich enough to get away with it. The work was too important to be endangered. Even the sacrifice of an innocent life was not too high a price.

Satisfied he had come to the right decision, Fendleman returned to work.

The Doctor lay stretched out on a grassy bank, by the side of a country lane, his hat over his eyes. He was dozing peacefully.

The walk through the wood had produced no sign

of a Time Scanner, or even of any building that might contain one. Eventually they'd come to this lane cutting through the forest and the Doctor had decided it was time for a little rest.

Leela, too restless to settle, had been keen to go off and do a little scouting around, and the Doctor had decided to let her go, warning her to stay out of sight. After all, he thought, she couldn't get into much trouble in the peaceful English countryside.

There was a soft call. 'Doctor? Doctor!' The Doctor opened his eyes and realised that he should have known better. Leela could find trouble anywhere.

Leela was standing over him. Beside her was a middle-aged man in farm-worker's clothing, holding an old bike. He was standing very still, probably because Leela had her knife at his throat. 'I have captured one of their warriors,' said Leela proudly. 'He came silently on this machine, and he is armed.'

The Doctor saw the old-fashioned bill-hook strapped to the bicycle-frame. He sat up and gave the terrified labourer a friendly smile. 'You must have been sent by Providence!'

Slowly the man shook his head. 'No, I were sent by the Council. To trim the hedges and cut the verges.' He spoke with a thick country accent.

'Your Council should choose its warriors more carefully,' said Leela scornfully. 'Any child of the Sevateem could have taken you.'

The farm labourer was balding and burly, with a look of sly, peasant-cunning. 'Escaped from somewhere, has she? If you're her Doctor, you didn't ought to let her wander round loose with that knife. She could do someone a damage.'

28

The Doctor said. 'You can put the knife away, Leela. I think the natives are friendly.'

'He wasn't hunting us then?'

'No!' The Doctor fished a crumpled paper bag out of his pocket and turned to the labourer. 'Have a jelly-baby?'

The man took the jelly-baby, nodding thoughtfully. 'You've both escaped from somewhere, haven't you?'

'Frequently!' said the Doctor cheerfully. 'Now then, what's your name?'

'Moss. Ted Moss.'

'And where are you from?'

'From Fetchborough village, about a mile away.'

'Fetchborough?' repeated the Doctor thoughtfully. 'Fetchborough . . .'

Suddenly he whispered, 'Tell me about the ghosts!'

Moss stiffened, and his hand went to something hidden beneath his shirt. 'Ghosts? Don't know what you mean. Nothing like that round 'ere.'

'He is lying, Doctor,' said Leela confidently. She had no idea of the point of the Doctor's questions, but the man's movement and breathing had betrayed him. Leela had an instinctive understanding of what the Doctor called 'body language', the way a person's movements reveal his true thoughts

The Doctor was thinking hard. If there was a Time Scanner in the area, it was presumably being maintained and operated by scientists. And in a rural community scientists would stand out . . . . 'Tell me about the strangers, then.'

There was an immediate response. 'Strangers? Reckon you mean Fendleman and that new lot moved into Fetch Priory?'

'Yes, that's exactly who I mean. Where did he come from do you know?'

Moss's fears were overcome by his love of a good slanderous, gossip. He lowered his voice confidentially. 'Well, that Fendleman's a foreigner, isn't he?' Moss produced this information as if it was sure proof of something sinister. 'Calls himself some kind of scientist. Businessman too. They do say he's one of the richest men in the world. Though you wouldn't think so to look at him, scruffy devil. They say he made his money in electronics. Don't seem likely though, do it? I mean, he ain't Japanese ...' Moss looked cautiously around and whispered, 'Some of his people dig up bodies!'

'Grave robbers?' asked Leela.

'Archaeologists, more likely,' said the Doctor. 'Where is this Fetch Priory, Mr Moss?'

'Far side of the village.'

'And it's haunted, of course?'

'Yes, but it's the wood more than the Priory that's——' Moss broke off, and again his hand went to the good-luck charm hidden under his shirt.

The Doctor lowered his voice to a sinister whisper. 'Don't worry, Mr Moss. We won't tell a soul—living or dead. Come on, Leela.'

The Doctor and Leela moved away, and Ted Moss stood clutching his bicycle staring after them. Thoughtfully, he began munching his jelly-baby.

Harry Mitchell glared furiously at the old country woman confronting him in the Priory kitchen. She was stout, shapeless and red-faced, with straggly

30

grey hair, and a wrinkled face like a winter-preserved apple. She was clutching an old shopping basket and she was in a towering rage.

Mitchell drew a deep breath, and struggled to keep his own temper. 'Just relax and stay here Granny. We'll get it sorted out.'

'Don't 'ee tell me what to do in my own kitchen!' roared the old lady furiously.

'This isn't your kitchen, Grandma!'

'And I baint your grandma,' shouted the old lady, her country accent becoming thicker with anger. 'So don't 'ee Grandma me!'

Colby and Thea came in at that moment, and were astonished to see their cook engaged in a furious row with a uniformed security man with a rifle slung over his shoulder.

'What's going on?' demanded Colby.

The old lady swung round. 'This feller tried to stop me coming to the house!'

Colby looked at Mitchell. 'This is Mrs Tyler, our cook. She lives in the gatehouse cottage. Who are you?'

Mitchell drew a deep breath. 'My name's Mitchell, and I'm the Security Team Leader. The house and grounds are under restriction. My instructions are no one gets in or out without clearance. This loony old trout seems to think she's an exception.'

'Loony old trout?' shouted Granny Tyler. Swinging her shopping basket like a club she aimed a wild blow at the security man.

More amused than alarmed, Colby moved hastily between them. 'Gently, Mrs T! Remember your varicose veins!'

Mitchell jumped back. 'I've had it with you, you

31

old stoat. Any more trouble and I'll have you outside and set the dog on you.'

Colby and Thea both sprang to the old lady's defence, both speaking almost at once. 'Now just a minute,' snapped Colby. And, 'You can't talk to her like that,' began Thea.

Suddenly calm again, Mrs Tyler shook her head. 'Don't 'ee mind him, my lovelies.' Her voice had taken on a soft, crooning quality and her bright eyes were fixed on Mitchell's face. 'He'll be sorry, sooner or later. Later or sooner he'll regret.'

Mitchell stood completely still as if transfixed. He had shrugged off threats from some of the toughest villains in London. Yet somehow the old woman's voice gave him a sudden pang of fear.

Granny Tyler's voice returned to normal, and the look of eerie brightness faded from her eyes. 'I'm a-goin' now. You can tell Doctor Fendleman I'll come back when that one is gone, and not before. I don't hold with the likes of him.'

She dumped the shopping basket on the table and moved towards the door, stopping for a moment to fix Mitchell with that unnerving stare. 'There 'int a dog born that'd go for me, boy. They got more sense than some people!' And with that she was gone.

Mitchell gave a rather uneasy laugh. 'Now I know why they used to burn witches!'

'Cheaper than oil I expect,' said Colby lightly. 'I don't know who you are friend, but I hope you can cook!'

'I told you who I am.'

'Then all that stuff about restrictions ... You really meant it?'

'That's right.'

32

'You said no one could get in or out without permission,' said Thea. 'Does that apply to us?'

'Yes, Miss Ransome.'

'But that's ridiculous!'

'Whose authorisation?' asked Colby.

'If I were you, sir, I should talk to Doctor Fendleman.'

'I think I will. You stay here, Thea, I'll go.'

Colby marched briskly along the oak-panelled corridor until he came to Fendleman's laboratory. He rapped then tried the door. To his surprise it was unlocked and he went inside. 'Now see here, Doctor Fendleman . . .' Colby broke off in astonishment at the complex array of electronic equipment all around him. He stood looking around, listening to the remorseless electronic ticking of the Time Scanner.

Suddenly Fendleman appeared. 'You are impressed?'

Colby jumped, and turned round, making an attempt to recover his usual coolness. 'Oh, I don't know. I always say, if you've seen one jukebox, you've seen 'em all.' He gestured around him. '*This* is archaeology?'

Fendleman took him by the arm and led him to the Time Scanner. 'This, Adam, is the ultimate archaeology. It was data from the Time Scanner which led me to choose the excavation site in Kenya. Once I had pinpointed the exacted location of the skull, you had reconstructed it, and Thea had dated it, then the real work of the Scanner could begin.'

'And that is?'

'To enable us to look back through Time itself!'

33

4

Horror at the Priory

The Doctor lay down in a clump of bushes, at the edge of the woods surrounding Fetch Priory. Leela had gone ahead to scout out the approach to the main gate. She enjoyed that sort of thing so much he felt it was a pity to deprive her.

There was the faintest of rustlings, and suddenly Leela was by his side again, her eyes shining with excitement.

'There is an armed guard at the main gates, Doctor. But do not worry. I will go and kill him for you!'

She drew her knife, and began to slither away. The Doctor grabbed her arm. 'Oh no you won't! Here, let me see.'

The Doctor wriggled after Leela. Soon he was close enough to see the massive iron gates of the Priory. As Leela had said, an armed security guard was on patrol, with a savage-looking dog on a leash.

'Shall I kill him?' hissed Lecla.

'No!'

'Why not?'

'Well, it would upset the dog, wouldn't it? Really, Leela, you must stop going round attacking people. You'll get us in trouble.'

'Do not fear, Doctor. I will protect you.'

'*You'll* protect me! Hah! We'll forget the front gate, Leela, and circle round the back.' The Doctor moved away. After a last regretful look at the unsuspecting guard, Leela followed.

Adam Colby was striding agitatedly up and down his laboratory. 'I tell you, Thea, Fendleman's as crazy as a bedbug. He actually believes he can see into the past with that electronic fruit-machine!'

Thea sat perched on a lab stool, looking as beautiful and as composed as ever. 'Did he demonstrate it?'

'Well of course he didn't demonstrate it! How could he? I mean, it's just a load of electronic garbage. He thinks because he can pervert the law of the land, he can do the same for the laws of science!'

'It's late for you to start being self-righteous about the law of the land, isn't it?'

Colby nodded miserably. After his initial protest, he had allowed himself to be persuaded to go along with Fendleman's decision to dispose of the body in the woods, and say nothing to anyone. 'Yes, I suppose it is.'

'Did Fendleman give any reason for not demonstrating this Time Scanner?'

'Apparently it only works after dark!'

'Minimising solar disruption?'

Colby stared at her. 'You're not taking all this nonsense seriously?'

'Fendleman's no fool when it comes to electronics. He's one of the authentic geniuses working in the field — or he was, until he developed this interest in archaeology.'

'Until he flipped his lid, you mean!' Colby opened the door. 'Come on, Thea, let's go and cook ourselves some supper.'

35

The Doctor dropped down from the top of the wall and a moment later, Leela landed cat-like beside him. It had been an easy climb. The wall was old and crumbling and there were plenty of foot-holds. He peered through the gathering dusk, getting his bearings. The Priory wall enclosed the edge of the woods, and although the trees and bushes were thinning here, there was still plenty of cover. A low ground mist was rising, and the trees had an eerie quality in the half-light, like shrouded figures, waiting. The Doctor shivered; he was letting his imagination run away with him. 'Come on, Leela, the house must be over there.' They moved away.

After supper, Thea rose silently from the table, and drifted away unobserved. There was a strange feeling in her mind, a feeling there was something she had to do . . .

She walked quietly along the gloomy oak-panelled corridors of the Priory until she came to Fendleman's laboratory, opened the door and went inside.

Inside the laboratory she stood still for a moment, listening to the faint whirr of the equipment, and the steady electronic ticking of the Time Scanner.

She had never been in this laboratory before, but moving as if in a trance she went across to the Time Scanner and switched it on.

There was a rising hum of power . . .

In Colby's darkened laboratory the skull stood on its metal column, staring into the darkness with empty eye-sockets.

At the precise moment that the Time Scanner was switched on, the skull began to glow, faintly at first and then more brightly . . .

The Doctor stood looking thoughtfully at Fetch Priory. The old grey building loomed like a castle in the darkness.

A few yards behind him, Leela heard a rustle of movement. Drawing her knife, she vanished in a patch of shadow. The rustle came again, and a hooded figure moved past her, heading in the opposite direction. Instinctively, Leela followed.

The Doctor whispered. 'We'll go and look for some kind of back entrance. Now whatever happens, Leela, stick close to me, do you understand? Leela?' The Doctor looked round, and realised he was talking to himself. 'She's done it again!' he muttered indignantly.

Blank-faced, as if in a trance, Thea stood before the Time Scanner, staring straight ahead. Moving as if by itself, her hand reached out and increased the power.

The electronic hum rose higher.

Leela tracked her quarry clear across the Priory grounds, to a thatched cottage which stood just inside the wall, not far from the main gates. She watched as the hooded figure slipped inside, then moved cautiously after it.

She wasn't sure what she hoped to find. But the

figure had been moving stealthily, determined not to be seen, and Leela had followed it as instinctively as a cat follows a mouse. She moved up to the cottage door.

Inside the cottage the hooded man was waiting. As experienced in the woods as Leela herself, he had soon realised he was being followed. Now he had led his hunter into a trap. He lifted down the shotgun that hung over the fireplace, took two cartridges from a box on the mantelpiece, and loaded the gun.

As the cottage door creaked open, he raised the gun and fired both barrels at point-blank range . . .

The Doctor decided to head for the Priory, hoping that he and Leela would eventually converge. As he got nearer to the building, he became aware of a strange sensation, a mounting sense of unease. There was a sound, very faint, on the edge of his consciousness, something not quite real. But it was there . . . A slurred, dragging sound . . . The feeling of strangeness, the vague unformed panic grew with alarming speed. Suddenly the Doctor realised that he could not, quite literally could not move. His legs refused to obey the command of his brain.

He heard the sound of the distant shot, and instinctively tried to move towards it, but he was paralysed.

Eyes fixed and staring, the Doctor stood motionless in the misty wood.

The dragging sound was still there, and there was something else. A hissing, gobbling *hungry* sound . . .

It was coming closer . . .

5

The Fendahleen

The Doctor drew a very deep breath and held it for a moment. He let it out, relaxing his body, emptying his mind of fear and panic. He began to sway gently to and fro . . .

Fiercely he whispered, 'Legs! Come on legs!' He took a few, jerky, stumbling steps. But they were taking him *towards* the unknown horror in the bushes.

'No, no, not that way—this way!' The Doctor swung stiffly round and began an awkward stumbling run. 'That's it, legs. Run! Left, right, left, right!' Moving like a wooden-jointed marionette, the Doctor stumbled towards safety.

Ted Moss threw back the hood of his old grey duffle-coat and stood peering at the half-open door, listening hard. Was his tracker dead? He'd fired both barrels at close range, but he'd heard no cry, and there'd been no sound of a fall.

Quickly Moss broke the gun, took out the used cartridges and reloaded with two more from the box. Raising the gun he moved cautiously to the open door and looked outside, holding the gun before him.

Leela was standing flattened against the wall, just to the right of the door. As the shotgun barrel appeared she sprang, grabbing the gun barrel, forcing it upwards, shoving Moss backwards into the cottage, wrestling the weapon from his grip in one smooth movement.

Moss staggered backwards across the room. An armchair hit the back of his legs and he collapsed into it. He looked up to Leela standing over him, aiming the shotgun.

'That shot will be your last,' said Leela grimly.

'I didn't know it were you,' moaned Moss.

'Well, you know now!' Leela's finger tightened on the trigger. She had always believed the only good enemy was a dead one.

'You was trespassing,' babbled Moss.

From somewhere behind Leela a soft country voice said. 'So were you, Ted Moss. Now, put the gun down, Miss.' Something hard and metallic jabbed her in the small of the back.

Leela stood very still.

'I said put the gun down!'

'Kill me, and your friend dies too!'

Moss went white. 'She's a nutter she is, Jack. She means it!'

The unseen Jack chuckled. 'He 'ent no friend of mine. So that's a chance I'm prepared to take. The gun, Miss.'

Leela lowered the gun and turned. Swiftly the man behind her took the gun, handing her something in return. Leela looked down and saw she was holding a wooden stick with a curved handle and a metal-tipped end—the 'gun' that had been pressed against her back. Angrily she threw it down.

The man who had tricked her broke open the gun, unloaded it, propped it in a corner, and turned to

40

face her. He was a young man, quite small, with a cheerful open face that had a rather mischievous quality about it. He wore an old green anorak, and a battered felt hat, like an upside-down flower pot. 'Now then, perhaps you'll explain what you were doing in my gran's cottage—*both* of you.'

In Colby's lab the skull was glowing more brightly now.

Colby himself was hurrying along the corridor, in search of Thea. Worried by her sudden disappearance after supper, he had searched the Priory for her without success. Now he was heading for the one remaining possibility—Fendleman's laboratory. He could hear the throbbing of the scanner as he approached. Maybe Fendleman was demonstrating one of his lunatic experiments for her.

To his surprise the door was unlocked. He opened it—and saw Thea, before the Time Scanner. 'Thea, what are you doing? Fendleman will go barmy, or barmier, anyway. if he sees you . . .'

Thea didn't seem to hear him. She sat before the Scanner in a trance, face blank, wide eyes staring straight ahead. Colby touched her shoulder, shook her gently. 'Thea? What's wrong?'

Thea continued to stare with vacant eyes. For her only the Time Scanner held any meaning.

In the kitchen, Mitchell put down his paper, swigged the last of his coffee, and decided reluctantly that it was time to go out and check the night patrols. Half of them would be having a quiet kip under some tree if he didn't keep an eye on them.

His attention was caught by a strange sound from outside. A kind of dragging, shuffling ... And there was something else mixed up in it, a sort of hissing, sucking, sound, with a chillingly hungry quality ...

Mitchell stood up—and found he couldn't move. His legs simply refused to obey.

The door burst open, and his face distorted in fear at the horror in front of him.

Mitchell screamed—and died.

Colby was frantically switching off the scanner. As the electronic whining died away, he heard a long echoing scream, from the direction of the kitchen. 'Thea, wake up!' he shouted. 'We've got to get out of here.'

Thea opened her eyes. 'Adam? What is it?' She looked round. 'What am I doing in here?'

'Didn't you hear that scream? It came from the kitchen.'

'What? What scream? What are you talking about?'

'Never mind!' He grabbed her arm and dragged her from the laboratory.

In the kitchen, they found the door to the yard standing wide open, and the dead body of Mitchell crumpled face down beside the table. Colby went over to look at it, and then recoiled. 'It's that chap Mitchell. Look at his face!'

Thea looked down at the dead man's face. It was frozen in an expression of unbelieving horror. She knelt beside the body. 'There seems to be some kind of blister on his neck. Could be a birthmark, I suppose,' she said casually.

(The tall figure of the Doctor appeared in the doorway, unseen for the moment by the others.)

'How can you be so dispassionate,' burst out Colby. 'The man's *dead*, Thea!'

Thea stood up, stared curiously at him—and crumpled to the floor. Colby went to lift her up, but the Doctor snapped, 'No! *Don't touch her.*'

Colby swung round, astonished.

The Doctor looked sombrely down at Mitchell's body. 'How many deaths have there been?'

'Two ... Now look——'

The Doctor took Colby's arm, pulled him to one side, nodding down at Thea. 'No. *You* look!'

There was a halo of light surrounding Thea's body, and in the air just above it, a shape was appearing. It was broad and flat, rather like a giant tape-worm, the fore-portion reared up like a cobra about to strike. The creature faded and vanished. Colby was shaken. 'What was it?'

'Well, I'm not sure—but it looked like an embryo Fendahleen to me ...'

'Embryo what?'

'Fendahleen. A creature from the legends of my own world. Supposed to have perished when the fifth planet broke up.'

'Do you know what you're talking about?'

'You saw it. If it's survived twelve million years the energy-reserves must be enormous.'

Colby looked sharply at him, thinking of Thea's mysteriously impossible dating of the skull in his laboratory. 'Why did you say *twelve* million?'

'What? Well, around twelve million. That's when the fifth planet broke up.'

'What does all this mean?'

43

The Doctor plunged his hands deep into his pockets, and stared down at Mitchell's body. 'There are four thousand million people on your planet and, if I'm right, within a year, there'll only be one left alive. Just one.'

Colby stared at him, sceptical but strangely impressed by the Doctor's quietly matter-of-fact tones. 'What are you—some kind of Armageddon pedlar? A wandering prophet of doom?'

'Who's in charge round here?'

'I am,' said another voice. Colby turned and saw Fendleman. He was covering the Doctor with a huge old-fashioned revolver. Stael and two uniformed security men were crowding the doorway behind him.

The Doctor whirled round. 'Ah, Doctor Fendleman I presume?' He paused for a second. 'Is that really your name, Fendleman?' Before Fendleman could answer, the Doctor was rattling on. 'Now listen, I want you to do two things. Dismantle your Time Scanner, and run some tests on Miss Thea here. Start with an X-ray of her skull . . .'

Thea was recovering by now and Stael assisted her to her feet. Her eyes widened at the Doctor's remark and she looked curiously at him. Fendleman raised the revolver. 'I will give the orders here.' He motioned to the security men. 'Lock him up in the storeroom.'

The security men came forward and took the Doctor by the arms. 'Is this the way you treat all your house guests?' he asked indignantly.

'Only the uninvited ones, whom I suspect of murder. Take him away!'

As the Doctor was bustled out, Stael rose from his

examination of Mitchell's body. 'It is just as before—the same mark on the neck . . .'

'This is a terrible thing,' muttered Fendleman. 'Terrible.'

Colby took Thea's arm and led her to the door. 'This time I *will* call the police,' he announced defiantly. 'Come on, Thea.'

Fendleman called after him, 'As you wish, Adam. But how will you explain why you did not call them the time before?'

Colby didn't reply.

Stael said quietly. 'Doctor Fendleman, the process of decomposition—it is much faster, this time . . .'

Ignoring the Doctor's protests, the security men bustled him down a short passage which ended in a heavy oak-panelled door. They opened it, shoved him inside, slammed the door shut, locked it and went away.

The Doctor yelled after them. 'Tell Fendleman there isn't time for all this!'

The footsteps died away. The Doctor looked round. He was in a tiny, windowless, square room, lined with shelves. Crates and boxes were stacked against the wall.

The Doctor sighed. It wasn't as if he wasn't used to being locked up. Sometimes it seemed the inevitable first step wherever he appeared. He usually managed to find his way out of captivity somehow or other. But the most terrible fears had been raised in the Doctor's mind, and if they were correct, every minute, every second, counted desperately. He felt like yelling, kicking at the door.

Forcing himself to be patient, he fished out his sonic screwdriver and set to work on the lock.

Jack Tyler sat sprawled out in an armchair, listening in pop-eyed astonishment as Leela stumbled to the end of her story. 'That do seem a bit far-fetched,' he said mildly.

'There 'ent a word of truth in it, that's why,' grumbled Ted Moss. He was hovering behind Leela, keeping guard on her.

Jack gave him a scornful look. 'How would you know, Ted Moss? You wouldn't know the truth if you tripped over it.'

Leela said calmly. 'Why should I lie to you?'

'Fear?' suggested Jack.

'Does it seem to you that I am afraid?'

'You ought to be!' growled Moss.

Leela ignored him. 'Well?'

Moss gave her a shove. 'I said you ought to be!'

Leela swung round and jabbed him casually in the solar plexus with her elbow. He fell gasping into a chair.

'I must go now,' she said calmly.

'Here just a minute,' called Jack.

Leela swung to face him, poised for attack.

Jack grinned disarmingly at her. 'Please?'

Leela hesitated. Jack Tyler went over to the chair, heaved Moss out of it by the scruff of his neck and gave him a shove towards the door. 'You! On your way!'

'I want to see Mother Tyler.'

'Well, *Mrs* Tyler, don't want to see you.'

'Where is she?'

'I dunno. Out somewhere.'

'Well, she's got summat for me. I paid good money for it.'

'Then you'll get your money back. Now get out.' Jack advanced menacingly. 'I said out!'

Moss stopped in the doorway and glared at Leela. 'I'll see you again—and when I do I'll settle with you.'

'Get some practice first!'

Jack grinned, and shut the door behind Moss. 'Nasty bit of work, Ted Moss. Him and some others from the village—well, I'm not sure exactly, but they do say they've formed a Coven. You know, Black Magic and that. The thing is, I'm afraid my old gran's mixed up in it. I mean, she's a good old girl really—but she were brought up in the Old Ways, see?'

For once Leela did see. Magic was still a familiar part of her mental world—despite all the Doctor's efforts. 'You mean the ancient magic of your tribe?'

'That's right. The old superstitions and that. You heard him call her "Mother Tyler"? Well, that 'ent because he likes her. That's from the Old Religion.' Jack Tyler frowned.

'Look, there's somethin' nasty going on round here. Do you know what it is? Have you and this Doctor bloke been sent to sort it out?'

Leela struggled to remember what the Doctor had told her. 'The Doctor came to stop the use of a . . . Time Scan.'

'And what's one of them when it's at home?'

'He says it will cause a direct continuum explo— no, *im*plosion!'

Jack gave an admiring laugh. 'You don't half tell some whoppers, don't you?'

47

'Whoppers?'

'Never mind. What about this Doctor of yours, do you reckon he'd help us?'

'I'm sure he would.'

'What's he like then?'

Leela smiled. How could you describe someone as complicated as the Doctor? 'He is very difficult sometimes—but he has great knowledge. And a kind of—gentleness . . .'

The Doctor took a flying kick at a box, sending it hurtling across the room. So far the simple lock had resisted all his efforts. The trouble was, it was too simple, thought the Doctor gloomily. A new triple-security electronic lock he'd have had disconnected in no time. But the old-fashioned metal contraption was too big and clumsy to respond to the sonic screwdriver. The Doctor gave the door a hearty kick. There was a tinkle of shattered metal, and it swung open. He must have weakened some vital part of the lock after all, and the kick had done the rest.

The Doctor hurried from the storeroom, hoping he wasn't too late.

Colby was marching up and down his laboratory. 'I should have gone to the police right away!'

'Then why didn't you?'

He gave a rueful grin, 'I've always been ambitious, Thea. That's a fault in anyone, and particularly in a scientist. When Fendleman offered me unlimited funds, I jumped at the chance. I owe him a great deal. When he asked for the body to be moved—well, it seemed so unimportant. But now, with Mitchell dead . . .'

'That's right, Adam, Mitchell's dead. So why don't you stop dithering and phone the police?'

'Right!' With a gesture of decision, Colby snatched up the phone. He listened for a moment, his face puzzled. 'There's no line. It's disconnected.'

'Disconnected?'

'Yes, as in cut off.'

'Adam, please can't you be serious for one moment?'

'I am serious. We're surrounded by guards, beset by wandering lunatics, and we've got a pair of corpses on our hands. On top of all that, the telephone appears to be very dead. We're trapped!'

A strange look came into Thea's eyes, 'It must have been planned!'

'By Fendleman?'

'No, not *by* Fendleman. But he's part of it. Doing what was planned *for* him. Don't you see . . . planned *for* him . . . that would fit . . . it would explain . . .'

'Explain what?' asked Colby uneasily.

'You haven't asked me *whose* plan it is. Ask me, Adam, ask me. *Ask me who planned it.*'

'Stop it, Thea! Stop it!'

Thea stared wildly at him. 'I did. Don't you understand? *I did!*'

6

The Coven

A little later, Thea Ransome sat pale and silent at the kitchen table, while Adam Colby raged about the room shouting at Fendleman. Stael stood silent in the background, listening.

Colby had decided to say nothing about Thea's outburst, putting it down to hysteria caused by the strain of the evening's strange events. But his feelings of unease remained, and they made the reproaches he heaped on Fendleman all the more violent. 'You must think my head zips up at the back!' he bellowed.

Fendleman remained infuriatingly calm. 'Be reasonable, Adam. Why should I disconnect the telephones?'

'For the same reason you've got the place surrounded by armed thugs!'

'And what reason is that?'

'Because you're *mad*, Fendleman!' Colby stopped short, as if realising that the charge made in the heat of his anger might actually be true. 'You're mad!'

Fendleman was toying idly with the big revolver, which still lay on the table before him. Smiling oddly, he picked it up. 'In that case, you are hardly behaving in a manner conducive to your own safety. I should be humoured, surely? Sit down, Adam.'

Colby sat.

Fendleman smiled, and pushed the revolver aside.

'I believe that the skull you have reconstructed is of extra-terrestrial origin.'

Colby laughed. 'An alien space traveller! Yes, of course. Hence the guards. You're afraid the next-of-kin will come to claim the remains. Expecting an attack by little green men from Venus, are we?'

Fendleman too became angry. 'Don't talk like a fool, Colby. You are not a fool!'

'No I'm not. That skull is human, a skull like yours or mine. Homo sapiens, modern man.'

'Exactly! And it is also twelve million years old. Millions of years older than the earliest of man's known ancestors. Suppose it is the skull of one of the *unknown* ancestors of Man?'

Despite himself, Colby was caught up in the astonishing concept. 'If that's true ... then we're *all* aliens ...'

Jack Tyler and Leela discussed the strange events around Fetch Priory for some time, without getting any further. Since Leela hadn't really understood the Doctor's explanations, Jack found it hard to understand hers.

At last he said, 'Well, let's go then, find this Doctor of yours. Perhaps he can sort it all out and make some sense of it all—if he's half as clever as you say he is ...'

Suddenly Jack tensed. He looked warningly at Leela, but she too had heard movement outside the door. Jack moved towards it, still talking in the same loud, cheerful voice. 'Yeah, if he's as clever as you say he is he ought to be able to sort it out——' He flung open the door in mid sentence. The consider-

51

able bulk of Granny Tyler tumbled into his arms. Her eyes were wide and staring, her face twisted with fear, her mouth open in a soundless scream.

The Doctor was moving cautiously along the corridor, when he heard voices coming from a half-open door. Incurably curious as always, he crept close enough to listen.

Tall and imposing in his crisp, white lab coat, Stael looked down at the cringing figure of Ted Moss. 'You should not have come here. There are security guards everywhere.'

'But I had to warn you . . . Besides, those guards are all town lads. Not hard getting past them in the woods at night.'

'It was a stupid risk. Fendleman is suspicious and uneasy. Why do you think he sent for the security team?'

'I had to warn you about the Doctor,' said Moss stubbornly.

(In the corridor, the Doctor raised his eyebrows, surprised to find himself figuring in the conversation. He edged nearer to the door.)

'There's a bloke calls himself the Doctor,' Moss was saying. 'Tall feller with curly hair. Got a girl working with him. I told them about this place—I didn't realise at the time, see. I tried to stop the girl, after. They know all about us! They're investigators. Come to investigate us, very likely.'

Stael listened to this confused babble with cold disdain. 'Whoever and whatever they are, I shall deal with them. Now go, quickly.'

(As the two men moved towards the door, the Doctor slipped away.)

Stael paused in the doorway. 'Are all our friends prepared?'

'They're just waiting for the word.'

'Make sure that all are ready. When the time comes, we must be twelve.'

Moss's voice became a kind of chant. 'You do lead the Coven now, but we know the Old Ways. Thirteen be the number.'

'A place must be left for the one that kills,' said Stael.

'It's circumstantial,' said Colby weakly. 'It's all circumstantial.'

Fendleman leaned forward. 'It is the only logical explanation, Adam. Man did not evolve on Earth!'

Thea Ransome sat silent, listening to the fierce debate between the two men. She felt odd, somehow detached. The old-fashioned stone-flagged kitchen seemed a strange setting for a discussion of the origins of Man.

Fendleman was talking quickly now, his long-suppressed theories pouring out of him in a flood. 'I am convinced that my theory is correct, Adam.' He paused impressively. 'There is something else that I have not told you. With the Time Scanner I have traced what I now believe to be the moment of death of this alien traveller. There was, at that moment, an enormous in-pouring of energy, the like of which I have never seen before.'

Fendleman's eyes were shining, his voice throbbing with conviction. 'This is what first attracted my attention. An in-pouring of energy, a concentration of power, as though to *store*.' Fendleman sat back, 'Now, I asked myself, *where* would this energy be stored—and *why*? These questions I could not answer—until I X-rayed the skull.'

'You X-rayed the skull?' asked Colby incredulously. When?'

Fendleman hesitated. 'Stael and I have been doing tests in secret for some time.'

'Oh thanks!'

Fendleman put a hand on his arm. 'No, no, Adam, you have a right to be angry. I should have told you all this before. But I wanted to be certain. Besides, from the very beginning I have had a feeling that this was so important that it must be kept completely secret.' He sighed heavily. 'Now we have these murders to contend with—and this mysterious intruder . . .'

Colby was struck by a sudden thought. '*He* said something about X-rays, didn't he? Wanted us to X-ray Thea's skull!'

Thea stood up. 'Will you excuse me, both of you. I'm feeling a bit tired. I think I'd better go and lie down.'

'You are looking a little pale, my dear,' said Fendleman absently. 'Perhaps you have been working too hard. I will ask Stael to look in on you later.'

Thea nodded. Stael was the only one amongst them with a medical qualification in addition to his other degrees.

As Thea left the kitchen, Fendleman said, 'It is obvious this intruder came to spy on us.'

'Well, yes,' said Colby dubiously. There had been

54

something very convincing about the Doctor. 'When you X-rayed the skull—what did you find?'

Fendleman rose. 'Come. I will show you.'

A blanket wrapped round her shuddering old body, Mrs Tyler sat huddled into her favourite armchair. Her grandson Jack was perched on the arm, and she was clutching his hand with a vice-like grip, and staring straight ahead of her, at some unseen horror in her mind.

Leela was trying to force some brandy into her mouth. 'Here, drink this, old woman. It will warm you.'

But Mrs Tyler would make no attempt to swallow, and the brandy trickled from the spoon out of the side of her mouth.

Jack Tyler wiped it away with his handkerchief. 'Gran? Gran, what happened?'

'Do not ask her that,' whispered Leela. 'It is because she does not want to remember what has happened that she is like this.' She leaned forward and stroked Mrs Tyler's forehead, and spoke in a low, crooning voice. 'You are safe now, safe. I will let nothing hurt you. Nothing can hurt you . . .'

The old woman began to mutter. 'I seen it . . . In my mind. Dark . . . great . . . it called me . . . in my mind. It called me . . .' Her voice rose in terror. 'It were hungry . . . hungry for my soul . . .'

'What does it mean?' whispered Jack.

Leela shook her head. 'The Doctor will know.'

'Nothing left . . .' said Mrs Tyler suddenly. 'There'll be no life left . . .'

Leela stood up. 'I must find the Doctor.'

55

'Help me,' moaned the old lady pitifully. 'Help me . . .'

Jack Tyler gave Leela an anguished look. 'Stay with her,' ordered Leela, and disappeared into the darkness.

As she left, she heard Granny Tyler's voice. *'It were hungry for my soul . . .'*

Fendleman held the X-ray plate to the light of the wall viewer. 'There? Do you see it?'

Colby studied the plate. 'Well, it *looks* like a pentagram, I agree. But it's just the way the fragments have been assembled, the pattern of the cracks.'

'No! That pattern is part of the structure itself. I believe it to be some kind of neural relay. That is where the energy was stored.' He put down the plate. 'It is interesting, is it not, that for as long as man can remember, the pentagram has been the symbol for mystical energy and power.'

Colby shook his head. Was Fendleman mad, after all? And was he just as mad for listening to him? 'All right, let's assume for the moment that's the "how", you've still got to discover the "why?"'

'A beacon.'

'A what?'

'Suppose the power is still within that neural circuit, and can only be released by the intelligent application of advanced technology?' Fendleman spread his hands. 'The release of that energy would act as a signal that there was intelligent life on this planet. Mankind would at last meet his——'

'Next of kin?'

'His destiny, Adam. His destiny!'

56

Leela came out of the woods, and saw a uniformed guard on patrol. She reached automatically for her knife, and then remembered the Doctor's views. Slipping ghost-like up behind him, she struck a quick, chopping blow. The guard fell. Leela caught the body, dragged it under the cover of a bush, and slipped inside the building. She felt rather proud of herself—she was really getting quite civilised!

Thea wandered through the corridors of the Priory fighting against a dark, alien force that seemed to be taking over her mind. Her mind was fixed on Colby's words about the Doctor. He'd wanted them to X-ray her skull. *He* knew there was something wrong with her . . .

The storeroom door stood ajar, and she called into the darkness. 'Please, are you there? I need help.'

There was no answer. Clearly, the Doctor had gone.

Thea wandered off, not quite sure where she was going. Her feet moved of their own accord, taking her to Fendleman's laboratory.

Colby and Fendleman had left, and the place was empty. She picked up the X-ray of the skull and studied it. The picture of the skull seemed to become the skull itself, burning, glowing, merging with her own, taking over her mind . . .

'Thea!'

She jumped and turned round. Stael stood in the doorway. 'Max, you frightened me. Do you have to creep about like that?'

'I apologise, Thea.' Stael closed the door and

57

advanced towards her. 'What are you doing here?'

Thea shook her head, not too sure herself. Then she remembered. 'I was looking for the stranger, the one who calls himself the Doctor. Do you know where he is?'

Stael shook his head. 'It is not important.'

'It is to me. I've got to find him. I think he can help me.'

'Why should you need help, Thea? The stranger has escaped—and anyway he can do nothing. It is too late. Too late for all the petty meddling fools . . .'

There was something very strange about Stael's manner. Suddenly Thea was frightened. She made for the door but Stael stepped in front of her.

'What are you talking about, Max?'

Stael smiled down at her. 'There is no need for you to be afraid of me. It is fitting that you should be the key to my power!'

For the first time she noticed that Stael was keeping one hand behind his back. 'Don't be such a fool, Max. Get out of my way!'

She made a sudden dart for the door. Stael slipped swiftly behind her, his arm came up, and a chloroform-soaked pad was clamped over her mouth and nose.

For a moment she struggled wildly in his grip, then slumped back, unconscious.

Stael lowered her almost reverently to the ground, and stood looking down at her.

'The chosen one!'

The Doctor was still lurking about the rambling corridors of Fetch Priory, feeling as if he were engaged in some lunatic game of hide and seek. He now had two problems, to stop the use of the Time Scanner, and to find some way of countering the even more deadly menace of the Fendahl, and he didn't seem to be making much progress. Three problems, really, since that fellow Stael was up to no good either.

It seemed pretty clear he'd get no help from Fendleman or the other inhabitants of the Priory. If they found him, he'd just be locked up again. He decided that the first step was to find and dismantle the Time Scanner and he set out to look for it.

His search took him to Colby's laboratory, where he found not the scanner, but the skull.

Unaware that it had any particular significance, the Doctor gave it a friendly nod, and looked round the laboratory. He tapped an exceptionally complex and expensive piece of equipment. 'Ah! Parastatic magnatometer. How very quaint!'

He picked up a bone from the bench and sniffed it thoughtfully. 'Mmm? Twelfth century, I think.' He perched himself on a lab stool, put his chin in his hands and stared thoughtfully at the skull.

The skull's blank eye-sockets seemed to stare sadly back at him.

'Ah, there, there, poor old chap!' said the Doctor sympathetically. He fished a paper bag out of his pocket. 'Here, would you like a jelly-baby? No, I suppose not!'

The Doctor was talking nonsense to dispel a mounting feeling of unease. There was something about that skull . . . Telling himself not to be so silly, the Doctor said, 'Alas, poor skull!' and patted it on the head.

The skull sprang to glowing life the second the Doctor's hand touched it. He tried to take his hand away, but it was locked, immovable.

The Doctor gave a roar of protesting agony as the power of the skull surged through his body, determined to swallow his very soul . . .

7

Stael's Mutiny

Leela moved cautiously into the empty kitchen, crossed it, and went through into the corridor beyond.

The oak-panelled corridors of the Priory were gloomy and silent. Leela was filled with a mounting sense of unease. She paused, almost as if sniffing the air, sensing danger. Somehow she knew the Doctor was nearby, and in trouble. Following her instincts, she hurried on.

Soon she became aware of a high-pitched noise, a kind of rushing of energy-sound. She ran towards it, and a few moments later she ran into Colby's laboratory.

With the last of his strength, the Doctor was desperately trying to free himself from the skull. Leela moved to help him, then stopped herself. If she touched the Doctor, might not the skull's evil power flow through him and into her?

She stepped back and kicked the Doctor's lab stool from under him. He fell, breaking the contact with explosive force.

The Doctor was catapulted across the room, slamming into Leela, and knocking her to the ground. For a moment he lay across her, a dead weight. Leela was afraid she had been too late. Then the Doctor stirred, and groaned.

Relieved, Leela said reproachfully, 'Doctor, you

are very heavy!'

Slowly the Doctor began getting to his feet. Leela helped him to rise, and he climbed painfully onto a stool. 'How did you find me?'

'I just felt something was wrong and followed the feeling!'

The Doctor smiled. 'Yes, of course you did!' he said affectionately.

'Have I saved your life?' asked Leela, pleased.

'Yes, I was careless.' The Doctor looked at the skull. 'You're becoming a mutation generator, aren't you?'

Leela gave the skull a horrified look. 'It's alive?'

'Yes, in a way. It's seeking appropriate genetic material to recreate itself.'

'But what is it?'

'I think it's the Fendahl,' said the Doctor sombrely. 'It exists and grows by death.'

'So do most creatures. You taught me that yourself.'

'Yes, but the Fendahl is insatiable, it can consume an entire planet. The Fendahl absorbs the full spectrum of energy, what some people call the life force, the soul.'

'That must be what the old woman saw,' said Leela suddenly. '"Huge and dark" she said. "Hungry for my soul".'

'Is she still alive?'

'Yes.'

'Take me to her!'

'What about that skull?'

'That's indestructible.'

'What about the Time Scanner?'

The Doctor hesitated. In a way, Leela was right.

But every moment they stayed in the Priory increased the risk of detection. 'First things first. Anyway, Fendleman can operate the Time Scanner for a hundred hours before there's an implosion.'

'Suppose he's already used up his hundred hours?'

'That's a risk I'll have to take;' said the Doctor exasperatedly. 'Now, come on, Leela!'

He realised he was still clutching the bone, tossed it onto the bench, and they hurried away.

Colby was still in Fendleman's laboratory, listening to his plans and projects for the Time Scanner. Now Fendleman seemed eager to talk, Colby was prepared to listen. Perhaps he would be able to decide if Fendleman was a scientific genius, or an obsessional madman. After all, suppose Fendleman was right? Colby didn't want to miss out on the greatest discovery in the history of science.

Half-lost in dreams of his Nobel Prize, he watched Fendleman check the reading on a digital clock.

'What's this then?'

'My running log, for the Time Scanner. It is necessary to keep a record. Some components have a limited life, and have to be periodically replaced.'

Colby checked the reading. 'Ninety-eight hours, fifty-six minutes, forty-three seconds! You've been busy.'

'It has been a joy,' said Fendleman simply

'A labour of love, even?' Colby picked up the X-ray of the skull. 'If man really is descended from aliens like this, why haven't we found evidence of it before?'

'Because we were not looking!'

'Oh, come on, now . . .'

'We were not looking for this sort of evidence,' insisted Fendleman. 'Without the Scanner, we would never have found the skull. With all research, Adam, there must be one vital first discovery. What is it the Chinese say? A journey of a thousand miles begins with a single step!'

'This isn't a step, though. It's a jump—and a jump to a rather illogical conclusion.'

Colby studied the Time Scanner with its triple bank of controls, and its complex array of monitor screens. 'Do you really think you will actually be able to see into the past with that thing?'

Fendleman straightened up. 'You shall see for yourself. I have already reprogrammed the computer. This time it should give us a visual interpretation of what the Time Scanner picks up.' He pointed to the big central monitor. 'On that screen, you shall see the true ancestor of Man!'

There was a hum of power as Fendleman switched on the Time Scanner. The digital recorder log automatically began its countdown.

Colby watched Fendleman as he hovered over the controls. Neither man was aware that, if the Doctor's estimate was correct, there would soon be a temporal implosion that would destroy their planet.

Maximilian Stael stood in the gloom of the huge Priory cellar, looking down at the unconscious body of Thea Ransome. At last the strange events of his tormented life were moving towards their supreme climax.

Stael was a man with a single obsession—power.

The only child of a distinguished Austrian scientist, he had been brought up by his scientist father. His mother had died when he was born. There was little love between father and son. Stael grew up lonely and aloof, unable to feel part of the rest of humanity.

Through the lonely years, Stael developed one bitter resolve. If he could not be part of humanity, then he would rule it instead. He developed a ruthless obsession with the search for personal power.

But how was he to achieve it? His coldness and lack of popularity ruled out politics. He soon realised that he had not the gift of true genius either in science or business. (Privately he hated and envied Fendleman, who had both.)

Stael's obsession led him, as it had led so many others, to the search for ancient secrets and hidden knowledge. It led him to Witchcraft and Black Magic, to the Old Religion.

He studied the subject with his usual determined thoroughness, and came to a strange conclusion. In certain times, and in certain places, magic worked.

Magic was a word for fools, of course. The truth was that there were ways of harnessing the psychic energy of the mind, of tapping the powers that ruled the entire cosmos.

Stael was still pursuing his hobby when he came to Fetch Priory to work as Fendleman's assistant. He had studied the legends of the area, the survivals of the Old Religion. He had made contact with Granny Tyler—and with the Coven of Witches that flourished in secret in the village. Before long he was its acknowledged leader.

Soon after he had begun work on the skull with Fendleman, Stael had worked out a weird religion of his own. It involved the skull, the Time Scanner, the psychic energy generated by the Coven—and Thea Ransome.

Stael stood looking down at her as she lay bound hand and foot before the altar in the old stone cellar that he had adapted as the temple of his rites. A huge pentagram had been painted on the stone floor, and Thea lay at its centre.

Stael bent over her, a hypodermic in his hand. 'Thea?' She opened her eyes and stared dazedly at him. 'Max? What's happening?' Her eyes widened with fear.

'I am glad you are awake, Thea. I want you to understand why you have been brought here. You are the medium through which the ancient power of this place is to be focused.'

'Max, what are you doing?' Thea began struggling wildly against her bonds.

'The Time Scanner awoke the power—you know about the Scanner of course? I have been watching you for some time, you see, Thea. You are the medium through which I shall conjure and control the supreme power of the ancients.'

Thea felt the slight prick of an injection, and almost immediately a wave of drowsiness came over her. 'Max, don't be so ridiculous . . .' she muttered. 'Let me go!'

'You will sleep now, while we prepare.'

As he turned to go Thea called feebly, 'Max, don't . . . You're a fool!'

'I shall be a god!' said Max Stael softly, and turned away.

The Doctor and Leela found a panic-stricken Jack Tyler still kneeling beside his grandmother. Granny Tyler sat motionless in her chair, eyes wide open staring into nothingness, an expression of fixed horror on her face.

He looked up eagerly as they came in. 'Is this him? Is this your man? My gran's in a terrible state!'

The Doctor leaned over the old woman. 'Mrs Tyler? Come on, Mrs Tyler, wake up!'

Leela joined in. 'Come on old woman, wake up!' She shook her shoulder.

Jack pulled her away. 'Leave her alone, both of you. What do you think you're doing?'

'Do you know what's the matter with her?' snapped the Doctor.

'Well, no, but . . .'

'Well I do! Make some tea.'

'Tea?' repeated Jack stupidly.

'Tea! She does drink tea?'

'Well, 'course she does.'

'Then make some. Use the good china, four cups, lay it out on a tray. Oh, and find some fruit cake. I love fruit cake.'

'Anything else?' asked Jack sarcastically.

'No! Don't just stand there, get on with it!'

Realising the Doctor was perfectly serious, Jack Tyler went through to the little kitchen.

The Doctor leaned over the old lady and shouted, 'Wake up Mrs Tyler! Come on, is this the way to behave when you're got visitors? We've come for tea!'

'And fruit cake,' added Leela.

'That's right,' shouted the Doctor. 'And fruit cake! He turned to Leela. 'I know a wonderful recipe for fruit cake!' he said loudly.

67

'You do?'

'Yes. You take a pound of peanuts and some apple cores . . .'

Fendleman pointed excitedly to the swirling vortex of patterns on the scanner screen. 'There, Colby! Do you see it?'

Colby couldn't really see anything, though he was too tactful to say so.

The arrival of Max Stael saved him from having to reply. To his astonishment, Colby saw that Stael was carrying Fendleman's revolver. He was even more surprised when he saw Stael level the revolver at Fendleman. 'Turn it off!'

Fendleman was still absorbed in his work. 'Where have you been, Stael? I needed you here.'

'Doctor Fendleman,' said Colby gently. 'I think you have an industrial relations problem.'

Fendleman looked up—and found himself staring down the muzzle of the revolver. 'What are you doing, Max? Have you lost your mind?'

'Turn off the Scanner!'

'No,' said Fendleman flatly.

Colby saw Stael's finger tighten on the trigger. 'All right, Max,' he said quickly. 'Relax, I'll do it.' He went over to the console and switched off the power.

Fendleman rubbed a hand across his forehead. '*Why*, Stael?'

'I am not yet ready. My followers are not here.'

'Followers?' said Colby admiringly. 'Well, that's impressive!'

'Shut up Colby, or I will shoot you now. Outside, both of you.'

Fendleman gave an uneasy laugh. 'Is this some sort of joke, Max?'

'I doubt it,' said Colby. 'Max isn't famous for his sense of humour—are you, Maxie?'

'I shall not warn you again Colby.' Stael gestured towards the door with the revolver.

'You're going to kill us anyway, aren't you?'

'That depends on whether I enjoy having you worship me,' said Stael seriously.

With a sudden chill of horror, Colby realised that Stael was completely mad.

8

The Missing Planet

Still speaking in the same loud voice, the Doctor was concluding his strange recipe. 'You mix the peanuts and the treacle, then add the apple cores, put them in a shallow dish in a high oven and bake it for about a fortnight . . .'

All the time he was declaiming this nonsense, the Doctor's eyes were fixed on Granny Tyler's face. It was fixed, immobile, like a waxwork face set in an expression of horror.

'It's too late,' said the Doctor sadly. 'She's slipping away . . .'

He rose and made for the door, Leela following.

Granny Tyler said sharply, ''Ere! Just a minute— that baint no way to make fruit cake!'

'Mrs Tyler!' said the Doctor delightedly.

Granny Tyler sniffed. 'Well, if you're staying, sit yourselves down then. I'll have the tea ready in a jiffy!'

Jack Tyler came in carrying a tray, his face one big smile. 'It's all here, Gran.'

His grandmother surveyed the contents of the tray with disapproval. 'But that 'ent the good china, John. And there's some fresh cake in the other tin.' She gave a sudden start, and glared fiercely up at the Doctor. ''Ere, what be going on? I never asked you to tea . . . I 'ent never seen you before in my life!'

The Doctor beamed, delighted with his own

cleverness. 'You were slipping away, Mrs Tyler. I needed something normal, everyday, to bring you back to reality. How long have you lived here?'

Granny Tyler's face became suddenly suspicious. 'Why should I tell 'ee aught?'

The Doctor nudged Jack. 'Tell her I'm trying to help.'

'He's only trying to help, Gran,' said Jack Tyler.

'You mind your place, John!'

Jack Tyler had been obeying his granny all his life, but he was in no mood to be bullied now. 'Oh no,' he said firmly. 'We 'ent got time for those games. Ted Moss and his cronies are up to something. Somethin' bad, and you're involved. Now, you just tell the gentleman what he wants to know.'

'I 'ent *involved* in nothing,' said the old lady with immense dignity. 'I were *consulted*. Lots of people consult me. You know I got the second sight.'

'You've lived in this cottage all your life, haven't you Mrs Tyler?' asked the Doctor.

'How do you know that?'

'Telepathy and precognition are quite normal—in anyone who spent their childhood near a Time Fissure, like the one in Fetch Wood.'

Jack Tyler groaned. 'You and my gran are as bad as each other. What's a Time Fissure then?'

'A weakness in the fabric of Time and Space,' said the Doctor solemnly. 'Every truly haunted place has one—that's why they're haunted. Time distortion, you see. This must be a large one, it's lasted long enough to affect the place names. Like Fetch-borough—fetch, an apparition.'

Granny Tyler peered suspiciously up at him. 'How come you do know so much?'

71

'I read a lot!' The Doctor became serious. 'What did you see in the wood, Mrs Tyler?'

'I didn't see aught—not with my eyes.'

'With your mind then. Did it have a human shape?'

The old lady said nothing.

'Did it have a human shape?' insisted the Doctor. 'I've got to know what stage it's reached.'

'No, it didn't.' Mrs Tyler clamped her lips shut, determined to say no more.

The Doctor stood up. 'Jack, will you do something for me? It could be dangerous.'

Jack looked worried. 'Oh! Well, if I can . . .'

'I want you to keep an eye on the Priory for me. I need to know who comes and goes. Leela and I have to go on a little trip, but we'll be back as soon as we can. Come on Leela, we've got a long way to go.' The Doctor hurried out.

As Leela followed, Granny Tyler called, 'Girl!'

'Yes?'

The old lady held out a tiny bag. 'Take this. 'Tis a charm to protect you. I cast it for Ted Moss—but 'tis too late for him.' There was a terrible certainty in the old lady's voice, just as if Ted Moss lay dead at her feet. Leela still hadn't lost faith in magic. She took the charm gratefully, and hurried off after the Doctor.

'John?' whispered Granny Tyler.

'Yes, Gran?'

'I seen that thing in the wood in another form . . . I seen it in one of my dreams.' She lowered her voice. 'Twere a woman . . .'

Thea Ransome still lay unconscious in the penta-gram on the cellar floor. Now Colby and Fendleman lay bound beside her. Stael checked that their bonds were secure.

'How long have you been planning . . . whatever it is you're planning?' asked Fendleman.

'Ever since I realised that Mrs Tyler's visions invariably came true.'

'Visions? Oh, come now Max. You have a first class brain. Use it.'

'First class brain?' jeered Colby. 'He's an occult freak remember. One of those poor fools who thinks he can speak with the devil. Is that it, Max? Are you going to summon up the devil?'

'Unlike you, I am not a crude and mocking lout, Colby. But spells and Black Magic incantations do not impress me. Mrs Tyler's paranormal gifts, the race memories she draws on—these were my sign-posts on the road to power.'

Colby yawned. 'Spare us the after-dinner speech!'

'I shall enjoy your terror, Colby,' said Stael coldly, and went away.

'I trusted him,' said Fendleman sadly.

'Well, I didn't,' said Colby bitterly. 'And I'm going to wind up just as dead as you—if that's any consolation.'

'Why is he doing this? Why?'

'Fendleman it doesn't matter why he's doing it. What matters to us is he's doing it—to us, unless we get free before his *followers* arrive!' A thought struck Colby. 'Hey, what about your Security Guards?'

Fendleman sighed. 'In my absence, they are instructed to take their orders from Stael.'

Colby groaned, and began struggling with his bonds.

The Doctor bustled Leela into the TARDIS, and began dashing frantically around the centre console. 'The fifth planet is a hundred and seventy million miles out, and twelve million years back, so we've no time to waste.'

· 'Why are we going there?'

'The Fendahl, as it is on Earth now, is already too powerful. I want to attack it at its origins, perhaps prevent it from reaching Earth at all.'

'Doctor, you say this thing . . . the Fendahl, comes from the fifth planet?'

'*Came* from it—a long time before Man developed on Earth.'

'How did it get there? You said there's only one of it. It can't build a spacecraft, so how did it get to Earth?'

'That's a very good question, Leela. I imagine it must have used its enormous stockpile of energy to launch itself across space.'

Leela tried to imagine some vast force streaking through the sky. 'Like lightning, you mean?'

'No, no,' said the Doctor. Then he considered. 'Well, yes, actually! Humans sometimes have dreams of astral projection, travelling psychically to some distant planet. That might be a kind of race memory . . .'

'Race memory?'

'Yes, you see sometimes people dream they've been to distant places. Or sometimes they think they've been before to places they're actually

74

visiting for the first time. "Déjà vu", you know?'

'No,' said Leela.

The Doctor sighed. 'Never mind,' he said, and went back to the controls.

Almost invisible in his old green anorak, Jack Tyler lay face down at the edge of the woods, watching the Priory. An old van drew up. Ted Moss and a number of other men got out and hurried into the house. 'That be the full Coven,' muttered Jack to himself.

He rose and slipped away.

It was hard to judge time inside the TARDIS, since it was travelling through time itself. The Doctor had explained that the TARDIS had its own subjective time, so that journeys seemed long or short just like any other kind of travel.

The journey to the fifth planet seemed a very long one to Leela. When the Doctor disappeared into some other part of the TARDIS, she dealt with her boredom by simply going to sleep.

Her dreams were confused and terrifying, and when the Doctor came back into the control room she was awake in a flash, her knife ready in her hand.

'No, no, put it away,' said the Doctor irritably. 'It's a good thing your tribe never invented firearms, they'd have woken with a start one morning and wiped themselves out!'

'There was something chasing me ... I couldn't move.' Leela yawned and stretched. 'Just a dream I suppose.'

The Doctor was carrying a pile of transparent

cubes. He stood studying them for a moment, and then hurled the lot across the control room.

Leela smiled. She rather enjoyed the Doctor's occasional displays of childish bad temper. 'What did you do that for?'

'I've been checking out all the old data banks. There's nothing in Time Lord records about the fifth planet ever having existed. Nothing at all!'

'Does it matter?'

'Well of course it matters! We Time Lords are a very meticulous people, you have to be when you live as long as we do. All necessary information is permanently recorded.'

Leela shrugged. 'Perhaps there wasn't any!'

The Doctor stared at her for a moment, and then rushed to the control console and activated the monitor screen. All it showed was a constantly rolling, weaving pattern of light. 'Of course. That's why there's no record of the fifth planet!'

'What is?'

The Doctor waved at the monitor screen. 'That pattern is a symbolic visual representation of a Time Loop—and we're caught in it!'

Leela was lost again. 'A Time Loop.'

'Yes! All memory of the planet has been erased by a circle of Time, making it, and its records, permanently invisible. Only the Time Lords could do that!'

'It's very clever,' said Leela tactfully.

'Clever? It's criminal! Though I daresay they had their reasons.' The Doctor began switching controls. 'We've been off on a wild goose chase, Leela, and we've got to get back. Let's hope we're not too far round the loop!'

Granny Tyler sat alone in her cottage, dealing out the Tarot cards, those ancient symbols with which she so often made her uncannily accurate prophecies. The fact that it was the middle of the night didn't bother her. As local white witch she was used to staying up all night, casting spells and charms at the proper hour.

She turned over a card, and moaned softly. 'The tower struck by lightning!'

Jack Tyler hurried in. 'Ted Moss and that lot be all at the Priory now. I just seen the last of 'em arrive. No sign of that Doctor then?'

Granny Tyler shook her head. 'Didn't think he'd be reliable. Never trust a man as wears a hat.'

'Grandad always wore one.'

'Aye, and a wicked old devil he were too!'

Jack pulled off his battered old felt hat. 'But I wear one.'

Granny Tyler's smile lit up her wrinkled old face. 'That be different,' she said triumphantly. 'I give it to ee!' She picked up one of her little bags. 'Here, take this.'

He examined it dubiously. 'More charms, Gran? I bain't one of your customers, you know.'

'Tonight is Lammas Eve,' said the old woman sinisterly.

Jack gave an uneasy laugh. 'You know I don't believe in all that.'

'Most round here do believe, and when most believe, that do make it so.'

'Most people used to think the world was flat,' said Jack defiantly. 'But it were still round!'

Granny Tyler chuckled. 'Ah, but they behaved as if 'twere flat!' She held out the bag. 'Come on, Jack

77

lad, just for me,' she wheedled.

Jack took the bag and stuck it in his pocket. 'All right, Gran, if it makes you happy.'

'And another thing. Gimme a couple of they cartridges.' Jack fished out the two cartridges he'd taken when he unloaded the shotgun. 'Going rabbiting Gran?'

The old lady rose. 'I be going to fill 'em with rock salt. Salt's best pertection there be!'

Jack took the box and tipped a handful of cartridges into his pocket. 'Evil spirits again, eh Gran?'

Granny Tyler looked solemnly at her grandson. 'You can laugh John, but I know the Old Ways, and I know the dangers—more than them up at the Priory any road. Soon as I've done these cartridges we'd best get up there, Doctor or no Doctor. We've got to stop 'em meddling in things they don't understand . . .'

9

Ceremony of Evil

It might have been a scene from the Dark Ages. Candles flickered on the great stone altar. The circle of black-robed figures stood waiting. It was as if a Black Mass was about to begin.

But there were strangely, modern elements in the scene. Besides the altar a small control console had been set up. A heavy power-cable ran out from beneath the console and disappeared up the cellar stairs.

Stael came down the stairs. He was carrying the skull, still mounted on its metal stand. Reverently he placed it on the altar. He took the gun from his pocket, laid it beside the skull.

Colby and Fendleman lay bound inside the pentagram, the unconscious Thea between them.

Colby nodded towards the console. 'What is that thing?'

'A remote control unit,' whispered Fendleman. 'It must be connected to the Scanner.'

'Your Time Scanner, Black Magic and the skull——' whispered Colby. 'What's the link?'

Fendleman had been thinking hard during his captivity. 'The power source,' he breathed. 'Colby, I think I know!'

The Tardis column rose and fell steadily, and the

Doctor stood looking at it in a frenzy of impatience. It had taken longer than he had expected to break free of the Time Loop. By now he was desperately worried about what might be happening back at Fetch Priory.

'We're going to be late!' said Leela.

'Well of course we're going to be late, it's obvious we're going to be late,' stormed the Doctor. He drew a deep breath. 'Sorry, sorry,' he mumbled. He stood for a moment, lost in thought. 'The question is, Leela, where is the Fendahl getting the energy from? Inducted biological transmutation takes a colossal amount of power, the kind that just isn't available in the Priory ... Aha!' The Doctor thumped the edge of the console, and gave a sudden shout.

'What is it, have you hurt yourself?'

'I've got it,' whispered the Doctor. 'The skull is absorbing the energy released when the Time Scanner damages the cosmic fissure. Why didn't I think of that before?'

Leela didn't feel much the wiser now that he *had* thought of it, but she was pleased to see the discovery had cheered him up. 'Never mind, Doctor, even you can't think of everything!'

'I can't?' The Doctor's face darkened. 'Well, I should have! But I was frightened, you see, Leela, by a horror from my childhood. Too frightened to think clearly ...'

Leela looked at him in amazement. Throughout all the dangers they had faced together, it was the first time she had heard the Doctor say he was frightened.

Maximilian Stael looked round the Coven. 'The waiting is over. Prepare yourselves!' He moved to the remote-control console.

Fendleman shouted, 'Don't do it, Stael!'

'Shut up,' hissed Colby beside him. 'Perhaps he'll electrocute himself!'

'You will kill us all,' screamed Fendleman. 'Listen to me, all of you. He is a madman! You must stop him now, before he plunges everything into chaos and death!'

'He'll plunge you into chaos and death right now, if you don't shut up,' muttered Colby.

Stael lifted the gun from the altar and walked towards them.

'Max, you just don't understand,' said Fendleman urgently. 'I know now what will happen!'

'You do?' asked Stael in a soft, mad voice.

'Max, you must listen to me. My name ... the Doctor asked if my name was real. *Fendleman*, don't you see? Man of the Fendahl. Only for this moment have the generations of my fathers lived ... I have been used,' screamed Fendleman. 'You are being *used. Mankind has been used* ...'

Stael raised the revolver.

Shotgun at the ready, Jack Tyler crept cautiously into Fendleman's laboratory. 'There 'ent no one in here either, Granny!'

Granny Tyler followed him into the room. 'That do mean the whole house is empty then, we looked everywhere else.' She peered suspiciously at the scientific equipment all around her. 'Don't hold with all this stuff, 'tis against nature.'

81

There was a muffled crack from somewhere below them. 'That were a shot,' said Jack instantly. 'Is there a cellar?'

'Great big cellar runs right under all this place. But it ain't been used for years.'

'It's being used now, then.'

Granny Tyler looked grimly at him. 'Come on then, boy. We'd best go see.' She hurried to the door, but tripped over the power cable that ran from the Time Scanner and out of the room. She stumbled and nearly fell.

Jack ran to help her. 'You all right, Gran?'

'What do you think?' she growled, and hobbled stubbornly on.

The Doctor and Leela ran boldly up to the main entrance of the Priory. The Doctor had decided things were too urgent to start playing Red Indians in the woods. There was no sign of any security guards. Stael had sent them all back to London.

The main gates were closed and chained. The Doctor cut through the big padlock with his sonic screwdriver, and they hurried up the drive.

Stael stood for a moment staring down at Fendleman's body.

'You murdering lunatic,' whispered Colby.

Stael ignored him. He turned and walked over to the remote-control console and stretched out his hand. For a moment he paused, savouring the power that would soon be his.

'The way to power is open,' he cried exultantly and threw the switch.

In Fendleman's laboratory, the Time Scanner sprang to life. There was a rising throb of power.

Granny Tyler hobbled down the corridor. 'Damn, boy, that hurts,' she muttered and came to a halt. Leaning his shotgun against the wall Jack put his arm round her shoulder. Suddenly she whispered, 'Ssh, listen, John. Somethin's coming ... *Somethin's coming* ...'

Down in the cellar, the skull on the altar began to glow fiercely. Brighter and brighter it grew ...

Dazed with fear and terror, Colby saw Thea Ransome beginning to stir. Strangely he had the impression that her body was throbbing with energy. Suddenly she rose, no *floated* to her feet, her bonds dropping away, and hovered in the air above the altar. A glowing halo of power surrounded her body ...

On the altar, the skull blazed with triumphant life.

The Doctor and Leela came tearing around the corner, and ran straight into Jack and Granny Tyler.

'Are you two all right?' asked the Doctor urgently.

'Just about. Damn glad to see you, though Doctor. Reckon you're not a moment too soon.'

'Moment too late, more like it,' grumbled Granny Tyler. 'Listen!'

From somewhere close by there came a muffled, dragging sound. (Around the corner a huge glistening body was sliding towards them, leaving a thick trail of slime . . .)

They listened. The sound came from the darkness at the end of the corridor.

'Come on,' said the Doctor urgently. 'Let's get out of here.' Nobody moved.

'Doctor,' whispered Leela, 'it's like that dream. I can't move.'

'It's my legs,' sobbed Jack. 'I can't move my legs!'

Granny Tyler pointed with a skinny finger. 'Look!'

The Doctor looked and saw utter, indescribable horror, gliding down the corridor towards them.

10

The Priestess

It was, thought the Doctor dispassionately, quite the nastiest looking life-form he had ever seen. In shape it was vaguely like an immensely thick snake, though the segmented front gave a suggestion of a caterpillar. It was green, and glistening, and it seemed to move on a trail of slime, like a shell-less snail.

The worst thing of all was the mouth. It was large and round, taking up most of the head—there were no eyes—and it was fringed with waving tentacles. From this mouth came a hungry, hissing, gobbling sound, as the creature slid towards them with ghastly deliberation. After all, why should it hurry? It knew they could not move. Like all its victims, they must wait, helplessly, to be consumed.

'Doctor, what's happening?' cried Leela. 'Why can't we move?'

'It's psychotelekinetic—controlling your muscles telepathically.' The Doctor found he could resist the control, just a little. With immense effort, feeling as if his legs were set in concrete, he began shuffling slowly towards Jack Tyler's shotgun, which was still leaning against the wall. As soon as he was near enough, he stretched out a long arm and snatched up the weapon.

'My old gun's not much use, Doctor. Only loaded with rocksalt.'

'No matter. The Fendahleen is already confused

because I can resist it. If we can confuse it a bit further we may be able to break the telepathic grip. Now listen everyone. Close your eyes, concentrate on your legs, and when I shout run—run!'

There was only a short distance between the Doctor and the Fendahleen now. It took every fraction of the Doctor's mental and physical strength to force himself to move down the corridor *towards* it.

He came closer ... closer ... With a sudden gobbling hiss of fury, the Fendahleen arched its back and lashed cobra-like towards him.

With a roar of 'Run!', the Doctor fired both barrels of the shotgun straight down the gaping throat.

The results exceeded his wildest hopes. With a throaty roar of agony, the creature writhed and twisted, and slumped squashily to the floor. The Doctor turned and ran, pushing the others in front of him.

In the cellar, the mutation of Thea Ransome was complete. She was no longer the pleasant young woman Adam Colby had known. Instead she was a gleaming, golden-robed figure, bathed in a glow of light. Her skin was golden too, and her spun-gold hair made an elaborate framework for her face.

The eyes were enormous, filling the entire centre of the face like those of some great insect. They were flat, blank, opaque, the eyes of Death. Thea Ransome was no longer a human being, but a High Priestess of the Fendahleen. Soon she would be the Fendahl itself.

Floating ghost-like through the air, the Priestess turned towards the robed, cowled figure of Ted Moss, who stood motionless in his place in the circle. She beckoned, and smiled a smile of dreadful cruelty.

As those great, shining eyes seemed to fasten on his face, Ted Moss gave a scream of sheer terror. 'No, don't do that. Please don't do that . . . No . . .'

Still screaming, Ted Moss sunk to the floor, shrivelled, and began to *change*. From his body there arose the writhing, undulating shape of an embryo Fendahleen. It began to grow.

The Priestess turned to a second member of the Coven. He stood helpless, awaiting his fate. 'Run, man,' whispered Colby. 'Why don't you run?'

Like Moss before him, the man shrunk to the floor. He too began to change.

Stael stood watching, horror-struck. 'No,' he screamed. 'No! This is not how things should be!' He tried to run forward, and found that he couldn't move.

In a corridor at the back of the house, the Doctor and the others came to a halt. Granny Tyler leaned puffing against the wall.

The Doctor surveyed his little party with pride. 'Well done, all of you. That sort of control is almost impossible to break.'

'What was it?' panted Jack.

Leela said, 'It was the Fendahl.'

'No, it wasn't,' said the Doctor. 'It was a Fendahleen, the one that killed the hiker and that security guard. It can only have been created out of pure energy, while the skull was restructuring Thea's brain.'

Jack looked at Leela. 'What's he on about now?'

Leela shrugged helplessly.

The Doctor noticed the power cable running along the edge of the corridor. 'What's that for?'

Jack shook his head. 'I dunno. Comes out of some big machine in one of them laboratories.'

'I reckon that do lead down to the cellar,' said Granny Tyler. 'I feel darkness down there—'tis like a cloud of evil . . .'

The Doctor said, 'Leela you'd better come with me. Jack, stay with your grandmother.'

'If you say so,' said Jack. Secretly he was rather relieved.

The Doctor turned to Leela. 'We'd better find out what's happening in that cellar.'

All but one of the rank-and-file members of the Coven had been transformed by now, and in their place stood a circle of writhing Fendahleen. The Priestess turned towards the final victim.

Besides Colby himself, only one human being remained—Stael.

Fighting against the paralysis with all his formidable will, Stael had actually managed to inch a few paces towards the gun that lay on the altar.

The Doctor and Leela slipped quietly down the cellar steps looking in silent astonishment at the glowing shape above the altar. Absorbed in the ghastly ritual of transformation, neither Priestess nor Fendahleen seemed to notice them.

Leela slipped behind Colby, clamped a hand over his mouth, and cut his bonds with her knife. 'Get him out of here as quick as you can,' whispered the Doctor. 'And whatever you do, *don't look into her eyes.*'

Leela began dragging Colby towards the cellar steps.

Colby struggled in her grip. 'What about Stael? We can't just leave him to *them*.'

'Leave it to the Doctor,' hissed Leela. 'Now, come!'

Stael saw them beginning to leave and shouted, 'Help me!'

'Come on, man,' yelled Colby. 'Get out now while you can!'

Leela took Colby's arm in a painful grip, and began running him up the steps.

The Doctor took a quick glance at the altar. Beside it an embryo Fendahleen was rising from the remains of the last member of the Coven. Soon the Priestess would be free—to turn her attention to *him*.

He hurried over to Stael, who managed to turn his head a fraction. 'Help me!' he sobbed.

The Doctor studied his face. 'It's too late, you've looked into her eyes.'

'The gun,' whispered Stael. 'Give me the gun. It's there on the altar.'

'Bullets won't have any effect on her.'

'No,' said Stael painfully. 'Not for her . . . for me!'

The Doctor hesitated. But even Stael had the right to die while he was still human. The Doctor edged slowly over to the altar, where the gun lay incongruously beside the blazing skull. He snatched it up and hurried back to Stael, pressing the revolver into his hand. 'I'm sorry. It's all I can do for you.'

An ironic smile flickered over Stael's face. 'Thank you.'

The Doctor turned and ran up the steps. As he reached the top, he heard a shot.

He turned and saw the Priestess, hovering over the dead body of Maximilian Stael. Her eyes were blazing with anger.

The Doctor ran from the cellar.

Leela dragged Colby along the corridors to where Jack and Granny Tyler were anxiously waiting.

'What's happening down there?' asked Jack.

'There are Fendahleen, everywhere . . .'

Colby slumped gasping against the wall. Granny Tyler gave him a look of concern. 'You feeling all right, Perfessor? You'm looking a bit peaky!'

Colby began shaking with rage and fear. 'This is all your fault, you silly old witch, do you know that? You started Stael off, you and your visions.'

Jack grabbed his collar. 'Just you watch your mouth, boy.'

Granny Tyler caught his arm. ''Tis all right, Jack, he's just frightened like the rest of us.'

Colby pulled free of Jack's grip. 'Don't you threaten me, you swede-bashing cretin.'

Losing her patience, Leela whipped out her knife and held it under Colby's nose. 'You nearly got us all killed down there,' she hissed fiercely. 'Now be quiet, or you will most certainly get yourself killed up here.'

Colby stood very still.

The Doctor came running along the corridor. 'All right, Leela, put that knife away.' He looked reproachfully at Colby. 'You nearly got us all killed down there, you know!'

Colby smiled wryly. 'It has been mentioned!'

The Doctor put his hands on Granny Tyler's

shoulders. 'The darkness you spoke of Mrs Tyler—the cloud of evil. Is it all around us yet?'

The old lady gazed into space for a moment, and then shook her head. 'No, not yet. 'Tis only down there, where you just come from. And 'tis not strong yet. It be getting stronger ... slowly.'

'Good! Now, let's go and look at that Fendahleen I assaulted.'

They made their way along the corridors, to the spot where the dead Fendahleen lay. If possible it was even more disgusting in death than in life. It lay humped and twisted in a corner. The green slimy skin had burst in several places like rotting fruit. The Doctor knelt to examine it. He seemed quite entranced. 'Beautiful,' he murmured. 'Quite beautiful!'

'Beautiful?' repeated Colby incredulously.

'I meant the effect of those rock-salt cartridges. Sodium chloride obviously affects conductivity, destroys the overall electrical balance, and prevents control of localised disruption of osmotic pressures.'

'You mean salt kills them!' translated Leela.

'That's what I said. It's probably the origin of throwing salt over your shoulder. Come on, Leela.'

The Doctor hurried away, and the others trailed after him.

He led them to Fendleman's laboratory, where the Time Scanner was still throbbing away. The Doctor stood in the doorway, surveying the machine with interest. 'How long had Fendleman been using this thing altogether?'

'I'm not sure.' Colby went over to the digital log. 'Here we are. Ninety-nine hours, fifty-six minutes exactly.'

'What?' yelled the Doctor. He leaped across the room and turned off the Time Scanner.

As the power hum faded, he leaned casually against the machine. 'Well, I've saved the world!'

Leela couldn't help laughing. The Doctor gave her a reproving look. 'Saved it from a Temporal Implosion, anyway. Unfortunately I was too late to stop the Fendahl. I'm afraid there's a very good chance this planet of yours is doomed!'

11

Time Bomb

It took Leela a moment to realise that the Doctor was quite serious. 'But we've already killed one of the Fendahleen. Surely we can destroy the rest?'

The Doctor shook his head. 'That was just a lucky shot, right down its throat. Not that it is a throat, of course.'

'Good marksmanship is not a matter of luck. You killed it, Doctor.'

'It was one isolated Fendahleen, Leela, comparatively weak. What's down in the cellar is the Fendahl. A Gestalt.'

Jack wondered if this was the name of some new and even more fearsome monster. 'A what?'

Colby was glad of the chance to enlighten him. 'A Gestalt is a sort of group creature. It's made up of separate parts, but when they come together they form a new and much more powerful being.'

Jack nodded to Granny Tyler. 'He reads a lot, you know—like the Doctor!'

The Doctor went on. 'The legends of Gallifrey, and the superstitions of this planet, make it fairly certain that the Fendahl is made up of twelve Fendahleen and a core.'

'You mean Thea,' said Colby sadly.

'Yes, but that thing isn't Thea now, any more than those other poor devils are——' The Doctor stopped short. 'Wait a minute! I killed the first one just now, so they need to create twelve in the cellar ... But Stael killed himself, so there can only be eleven ...'

Leela grasped what he was getting at. 'You are saying the Fendahl is not complete?'

'Exactly! Which means that we still have a chance!' The Doctor looked thoughtfully at the Time Scanner, a plan already forming in his mind. 'I'll need time, though ... Jack, have you got any more of those salt-filled cartridges?'

Jack fumbled in the pockets of his anorak. ''Fraid not. Got some ordinary ones, that's all.'

'Then we need some more rock salt—quickly.'

''Ere!' said Granny Tyler suddenly. 'You two still got they charms I gave you?'

Jack and Leela produced the two little bags.

'Empty 'em out,' ordered the old lady.

Leela found an empty glass dish, and they began tipping the little bags into it.

'Often wondered what was in these charms of yours, Gran,' said Jack teasingly.

'Rock salt!' said Granny Tyler. A little shame-facedly she added, 'Salt were always a powerful charm!'

The Doctor said, 'Jack, you get on with fixing those cartridges.' Hurriedly Jack set to work. 'Mrs Tyler, I want you to collect all the salt in the house, table salt, cooking salt, anything you can find. Fill as many containers as you can.'

'Right you are,' said Mrs Tyler sturdily, and hobbled away.

Soon, Jack had finished working on two more cartridges. The pellets of lead shot had been replaced with salt. The Doctor went over to him. 'Jack, you must be very careful to do exactly as I say.

94

Go out into the corridor and keep watch while I work in here. If you see a Fendahleen, don't hang around. Just give it both barrels and run. Now, off you go.'

Jack Tyler reloaded the shotgun. Pale but determined, he took up his post in the corridor. The Doctor looked thoughtfully after him. 'I think you'd better go too, Leela.' Something told him Jack Tyler could use the help of Leela's fighting spirit.

The Doctor produced his sonic screwdriver, removed a panel and began dismantling the Time Scanner.

In the cellar, the golden Priestess floated phantom-like above the altar.

On the altar itself the skull still glowed, not with the same fierce blaze as before, but brightly enough. It had been deprived of the energy produced by the use of the Time Scanner but by now it had ample in store to carry out its task.

Slowly the shimmering, half-transparent form of another Fendahleen appeared on the altar. It was tiny as yet. It would take some time to materialise fully, and then to grow. The Fendahleen lived by death, and, at this delicate embryo stage, they flourished best if fed with a human life. For the moment there were no more lives available.

The energy flowed from the skull, feeding the embryo Fendahleen. When it was strong enough, it would go out and seek nourishment for itself.

Above the altar, the Priestess floated, waiting, huge eyes staring fixedly at the skull. Once there were twelve mature Fendahleen to merge with her, she would become the Fendahl—and no force on Earth would be able to stand against her.

There was not long to wait.

Colby sat on a lab stool, watching the Doctor dismantle the Time Scanner. He seemed to have taken most of the vital parts out of its innards, and he was now reassembling them in a different order.

Colby thought how outraged Fendleman would have been to see his precious apparatus handled in this way. Not that Fendleman was in a position to worry any longer. He had died in the cellar, killed by the madman Stael—who had himself died by the same gun.

Colby rubbed a hand wearily across his eyes. Stael dead, Fendleman dead, Thea transformed into some unearthly alien being. He was the only survivor—and all because of the incredible sequence of events the Doctor had been telling him about.

Colby drew a deep breath. 'Let me just go over all this again, Doctor, to make sure I've got it right. You say that about twelve million years ago on a nameless planet which no longer exists, evolution went up a blind alley?'

Head buried in the Scanner, the Doctor gave an encouraging grunt.

'Natural selection turned back on itself. A creature evolved which prospered by absorbing the energy waves of life itself?'

'Um!' said the Doctor encouragingly, still inside the machine.

'So this thing ate life, all life, even that of its own kind?'

The Doctor's head popped out. 'That's right. In other words—the Fendahl. My people, the Time Lords, got wind of it. To prevent the thing spreading throughout the universe, they decided to destroy the whole planet, and hide the facts from posterity.'

'Quite an operation.'

The Doctor nodded. 'Between you and me, they don't usually do that sort of thing. They must have been a bit more enterprising in those days!'

'However, when these Time Lords of yours acted, it was already too late. The Fendahl had already come here, to Earth?'

'That's right! Mind you, it probably took in Mars on the way. That's why it's a dead planet.'

'But when it arrived here, somehow it got itself buried—but not dead?'

'The Fendahl *is* death,' said the Doctor. 'How do you kill death itself?'

He fitted a minute electronic circuit into place. 'No, what happened is, the latent energy amassed by the Fendahl was stored in the skull, and then sent out as a biological transmutation field. Any intelligent life-form that came within the field was influenced to evolve into something the Fendahl could use.

Colby's mind recoiled from the next logical step. 'Are you saying that skull created man?'

'No. But I am saying that it may well have affected his evolution. That would explain the darker side of man's nature. Just a theory of course!'

'A pretty wild one, too, Doctor.'

The Doctor grinned. 'More fun that way!' He began fitting the panel back onto the Time Scanner.

Outside in the corridor, Leela whispered. 'Listen!'

Jack raised his shotgun. 'What? I can't hear nothing!'

'Sssh! There's something coming, moving this way.' Leela turned to Jack. 'Remember what the Doctor said. As soon as you see it—fire!'

Jack was staring wide-eyed over her shoulder. 'Look!'

Leela looked. The Fendahl Priestess was floating eerily down the corridor towards them.

There was a Fendahleen at her side.

Jack Tyler had been braced for the horror of the Fendahleen itself, but the glowing golden figure of the Priestess seemed to hypnotise him.

'Don't look into her eyes, Jack,' whispered Leela. *'Fire the gun!'*

Jack took a stumbling step towards the Priestess, gun-barrel wavering wildly. 'I can't,' he sobbed. 'I got to . . . I got to . . .'

Fendahl and Priestess glided slowly nearer.

'Jack, give me the gun!' shouted Leela.

Jack Tyler stood there, frozen. He took another step towards the Priestess. The Fendahleen roared hungrily. Leela struck a short chopping blow to his neck, and grabbed the gun as he fell.

She tried to swing it up to cover the Fendahleen, but to her horror she could hardly move it. Already she was affected by the paralysis.

Inch by painful inch, Leela forced herself to raise the gun-barrel.

The Doctor finished putting the panel in place. 'There, that's it.' He grinned mischievously at

Colby. 'Of course, if you want an alternative explanation, the Fendahl built into the brains of some individuals the instincts and compulsions necessary to bring about its re-creation. They were passed through the generations until they reached Fendleman and people like him.'

'That's a little more plausible . . .'

'Or on the other hand, it could all be coincidence,' said the Doctor cheerily. 'Right, that's finished!'

They heard the roar of a shotgun. The Doctor gripped Colby's arm. 'Things are warming up. Go and find me a nice big lead-lined box will you?'

As Colby ran from the room, the Doctor took a last look at the Time Scanner, and switched the digital recorder back to zero.

He watched the figures whirl round the dial, spinning from ninety-nine hours to zero. 'Time's running out,' said the Doctor thoughtfully. He hurried from the room.

In the centre of the pentagram, the golden figure of the Priestess materialised amidst the waiting Fendahleen.

The skull on the altar glowed brighter—and suddenly yet another embryo Fendahleen began to materialise.

The Doctor found three bodies sprawled out in the corridor, though only one of them was dead. Jack was sitting slumped against the wall. He was rubbing his neck, and trying to sit up.

Leela lay flat on her back in the middle of the

corridor, shotgun clasped to her chest. Beyond her was the shattered body of a Fendahleen. The Doctor ran over to her. 'Leela? Are you all right?'

She opened her eyes. 'Doctor? What happened? Did I hit it?'

The Doctor beamed at her. 'Yes, yes, you most certainly did. You were quite right, good marksmanship isn't just a matter of luck.' He helped her to her feet. 'Come on, we've got work to do!' Jack was on his feet by now, and the Doctor said, 'Mr Tyler, I think we should go and find your granny!'

In the cellar the skull glowed on the altar.

The Priestess hovered in the pentagram, waiting.

The embryo Fendahleen grew larger, stronger.

Soon all would be ready.

Minutes later they all converged on Fendleman's laboratory, Granny Tyler pushing a tea trolley laden with cups, jars, boxes, containers of every kind, each with its ration of salt. A shopping basket was perched on top of them.

'There you are, all the salt I could lay me hands on.'

'Excellent! Battle stations everyone. Leela, you fill that basket with salt containers. Jack, I think you'd better take Mrs Tyler back to the cottage. You've done all you can here.'

Jack nodded. 'If you say so, Doctor.' He took his grandmother's arm and led her off.

Colby met them in the doorway. He was carrying a large metal box. 'Hey where are you two off to?'

'See you later, back at the cottage,' said Jack hurriedly.

Granny Tyler gave him a beaming smile. 'You'll catch up with us then, will you Perfessor?'

'Don't worry, I'll probably overtake you!'

The Tylers went out. Colby handed the Doctor the box. 'There you are, Doctor, one lead-lined box as ordered!'

The Doctor examined it. 'Perfect. All right, then, here's what you do. Give Leela and me time to reach the cellar—then start the Time Scanner again. I've modulated the beam, and with luck that should confuse things long enough for us to grab the skull and get out.'

'What do I do next?'

'Ah, the next bit's very important. Whatever you do, be sure not to operate the Scanner for more than two minutes. Then switch off and get out of the Priory.'

'All right. But why?'

'I've rigged the Time Scanner so as to set off a controlled implosion three minutes *after* it's next used and switched off. It's not so much a Time Scanner now, as a Time Bomb! We'll all need that three minutes to get safely out of range.'

'Ah! A big bang?'

'Pretty big,' said the Doctor cheerfully. 'Big enough to smash everything in this place to atoms!'

'Why don't we just leave the skull here, then?' asked Leela. 'It would be destroyed with everything else.'

'Too dangerous. It could survive, pop up later and start the whole thing over again.'

The Doctor pushed her towards the door.

101

'Good luck,' said Leela. She gave Colby an unexpected peck on the cheek.

He stood rubbing his face wonderingly as they disappeared.

Seconds later the Doctor's head popped back in again. 'Now remember, Colby—three minutes to get clear!' He disappeared again.

Colby went to the Time Scanner and stood waiting. He imagined the Doctor and Leela moving through the corridors at the back of the Priory, down the cellar steps . . . He wondered what horrors they would have to face. They must be there by now, he decided.

With a muttered 'Right!' he switched on the Time Scanner.

On the digital log, seconds began ticking away.

12

The End of the Fendahl

The Doctor and Leela paused at the top of the cellar steps, looking at the weird scene below.

It was a fascinating and horrible sight.

The enormous cellar was lit only by the glow of the skull upon the altar, and the golden radiance that flowed from the Priestess as she hovered wraith-like above the pentagram.

All around in the darkness were the undulating, slug-like forms of the Fendahleen. The air was full of the restless sounds of their heavy, slithering bodies.

The Doctor and Leela began creeping cautiously down the steps, the Doctor in the lead. Leela clutched the shopping basket under her left arm, a jam-jar full of salt ready in her right hand. The Doctor had the lead-lined box, clutched close to his body.

Leela made to move forward, but the Doctor stopped her. 'Not yet—wait for Colby to switch on the Time Scanner.'

The minutes dragged on endlessly. Leela wondered how long it would be before the Priestess became aware of their presence and sent her Fendahleen to destroy them.

Suddenly the light from the skull began to pulse irregularly. The snake-like bodies of the Fendahleen began weaving agitatedly to and fro. The hovering

Priestess was spinning and turning in agitated flurries of movement.

'Now!' whispered the Doctor.

The Doctor counted eleven Fendahleen around the altar. On the altar itself was a twelfth, not yet fully developed. When it was mature, the Gestalt would be complete, and the Fendahl invincible.

The Doctor had to pass very close to a Fendahleen on his way to the altar. Suddenly the creature seemed to become aware of him. It swung round, hissing hungrily, and the gaping mouth lunged down.

'Look out, Doctor,' called Leela, and hurled her jar. It shattered, showering the Fendahleen with glass and rock salt. It hissed and slithered back. The Doctor slipped by, calling over his shoulder. 'Don't forget to save some for the way back.'

'Do not worry, Doctor!' Leela had another jar ready in her hand.

The Doctor reached the altar. He put the box down close to the skull, and opened the lid. Beside him, the embryo Fendahleen weaved and undulated on the altar.

The Doctor waited, poised. When the Time Scanner was switched off again, there would be one precious second . . .

Colby's eyes were fixed on the digital clock, his finger on the Time Scanner's power switch.

The clock read 1.55. One minute, fifty-five seconds. Colby watched the figures change. 1.56, 1.57, 1.58, 1.59 . . . He threw the switch.

'Right, Doctor, you've got three minutes!'
Colby turned and ran.

The glow of the skull pulsed brighter, and faded for a second—and in just that second the Doctor snatched it up, dropped it into the box and slammed down the lid.

'Got it!' he yelled. 'Let's get out of here!'

All around them, the hissing and slithering of the Fendahleen had stopped. It began again, a rising, more threatening note.

'What's happening?' shouted Leela.

'Colby's switched off the scanner beam. We've got three minutes. Come on.'

They turned and ran for the steps. Leela paused at the top, threw a couple more salt-jars at the seething Fendahleen, and ran on after the Doctor.

They tore along the corridors at frantic speed until they turned into the main passage that led to the front door.

'Look,' screamed Leela, dropping her basket. The Priestess floated in mid-air before them, barring their way.

For a moment the Doctor thought everything was lost. Then he saw that the outline of the Priestess was pulsating, flickering . . .

'No, *don't* look!' he yelled.

Leela at his heels he ran head down, straight *through* the golden figure.

They shot through the open front door into pitch black night.

'We've done it!' yelled Leela triumphantly.

'Never mind the celebrations—just keep running!'

105

Clutching the heavy metal box, the Doctor sprinted for the woods.

Pulsing and flickering erratically, the Priestess materialised above the altar.

She vanished, reappeared on the stairs, vanished again, and materialised in the centre of the pentagram.

She sank slowly to her knees, the wide eyes staring with a curious pathos. Suddenly she disappeared into a vortex of whirling light.

All around the Fendahleen hissed and gobbled hungrily.

In the darkness of the woods the Doctor suddenly realised he couldn't see Leela. 'Leela, where are you?'

She materialised at his side, like a shadow. 'I'm here, Doctor.'

The Doctor smiled. He should have realised it was practically impossible to lose Leela in the woods at night. He did a mental time-check. 'Keep running, Leela, there's not long to go!'

They ran on, till the reassuring blue shape of the TARDIS appeared amidst the trees.

In the cottage, Jack Tyler and his gran collapsed gasping for breath. Jack looked concernedly at the old lady. 'You all right, Gran?'

She nodded, too winded to speak.

Jack listened. 'Someone's coming!'

Colby shot through the door and dived straight under the table. 'Come on, you two, get your heads down!'

Jack grabbed the old lady's arm, and pulled her protesting beneath the big table.

All three crouched down.

Colby looked at his watch. 'Any minute now!'

The cottage shook to the roar of a colossal explosion.

Fetch Priory vanished in a sudden uprush of smoke and flame, a roaring column of fire.

Then something very strange happened. The explosion coiled in and down upon itself, became the controlled *imp*losion that the Doctor had planned.

The smoke and flame spun into a rushing vortex and disappeared, leaving a charred and smoking circle of blackened ground.

Fetch Priory had vanished.

The Doctor and Leela paused by the TARDIS, listening to the uncanny silence as the explosion died away.

'What now?' asked Leela.

'We leave,' said the Doctor promptly. 'Vanishing priories take a lot of explaining!'

'Will the others be all right?'

'Oh yes. They're probably at Mrs Tyler's by now, eating plum cake off her best china.'

He opened the TARDIS door.

In the cottage, the trio beneath the table raised their heads. Weary as she was, Granny Tyler gave a sudden radiant smile. Somehow she sensed that the alien evil which had gathered over Fetch Priory was gone forever.

Adam Colby drew a long, sobbing breath of relief, jubilant and guilty at the same time that of all those who had worked at Fetch Priory, he was the only one left alive.

Jack Tyler mopped his brow and said plaintively, 'Put the kettle on, Gran, eh?'

The TARDIS was in flight through the vortex of Space/Time. The Doctor hovered over the navigational controls, and Leela looked at the lead-lined box, which he'd balanced casually on top of the console.

'What are we going to do about the skull?'

'Look for a star about to go super-nova and then dump it in the middle.'

'And that will destroy it?'

'Oh yes! I don't think even that skull can survive the temperatures generated by a super-nova!' The Doctor gave a grunt of satisfaction. 'Found one—in the constellation of Canthares. I'll just set the co-ordinates, and we're on our way.'

'*Then* what are we going to do?'

The Doctor peered at her over the console. 'I like your new outfit.'

'It's the old one.'

'Yes, it has a certain . . .' His voice trailed off, as he concentrated on the tricky business of astronavigation.

'A certain what?'

'What?'

'You didn't finish, Doctor.'

'Finish what?'

'Your sentence! It's a very annoying habit, Doctor.'

'I've been thinking about K . . . er . . .' announced the Doctor vaguely.

'K9?'

The Doctor nodded. 'K9! I'd better finish repairing him, hadn't I?'

Leela gave a little cry of triumph. 'Ah! You called him *him*.'

'I can call K9 him if I want to! He's my dog—aren't you K9?'

To the Doctor's astonishment and delight, K9 slowly nodded his head, and gave a faint but cheerful beep.

Leela smiled, the Doctor laughed, and the TARDIS sped on its way to new adventures.

'DOCTOR WHO'

0426112792	**TERRANCE DICKS** **Doctor Who and The Giant Robot**	**95p**
0426112601	**Doctor Who and The Genesis of the Daleks**	**95p**
0426201310	**Doctor Who and The Horns of Nimon**	**85p**
0426200772	**Doctor Who and The Image of Fendhal**	**£1.25**
0426200934	**Doctor Who and The Invasion of Time**	**95p**
0426200543	**Dr Who and The Invisible Enemy**	**£1.25**
0426201485	**Doctor Who and The Keeper of Traken**	**£1.25**
0426201256	**PHILIP HINCHCLIFFE** **Doctor Who and The Keys of Marinus**	**85p**
0426201477	**DAVID FISHER** **Doctor Who and The Leisure Hive**	**£1.25**
0426201493	**CHRISTOPHER H BIDMEAD** **Doctor Who – Logopolis**	**£1.25**
0426118936	**PHILIP HINCHCLIFFE** **Doctor Who and The Masque of Mandragora**	**85p**
0426201329	**TERRANCE DICKS** **Doctor Who and The Monster of Peladon**	**85p**
16909	**Doctor Who and The Mutants**	**£1.25**
	Doctor Who and The Nightmare of Eden	**85p**
	Who and The the Daleks	**£1.25**
		£1.25
		95p
		lteration

'DOCTOR WHO'

0426200373	TERRANCE DICKS **Doctor Who and The** **Android Invasion**	**90p**
042611471X	MALCOLM HULKE **Doctor Who and** **The Cave Monsters**	**£1.25**
0426110250	TERRANCE DICKS **Doctor Who and** **The Carnival of Monsters**	**£1.25**
042620123X	DAVID FISHER **Doctor Who and The** **Creature from the Pit**	**90p**
0426113160	DAVID WHITAKER **Doctor Who and The Crusaders**	**£1.25**
0426114981	BRIAN HAYLES **Doctor Who and The Curse** **of Peladon**	**75p**
0426114639	GERRY DAVIS **Doctor Who and The Cybermen**	**85p**
0426113322	BARRY LETTS **Doctor Who and The Daemons**	**£1.50**
042611244X	TERRANCE DICKS **Doctor Who and The Dalek** **Invasion of Earth**	**£1.25**
0426103807	**Doctor Who and The Day** **of the Daleks**	**85p**
0426119657	**Doctor Who and** **The Deadly Assassin**	**£1.25**
042620042X	**Doctor Who – Death to** **the Daleks**	**£1.25**
0426200969	**Doctor Who and the** **Destiny of the Daleks**	**90p**
0426103726	MALCOLM HULKE **Doctor Who and** **The Doomsday Weapon**	**£1.25**
0426200063	TERRANCE DICKS **Doctor Who and The Face of Evil**	**£1.25**
0426201507	ANDREW SMITH **Doctor Who Full Circle**	**£1.25**

STAR Books are obtainable from many booksellers and newsagents. If you have any difficulty please send purchase price plus postage on the scale below to:-

Star Cash Sales
P.O. Box 11
Falmouth
Cornwall
OR
Star Book Service,
G.P.O. Box 29,
Douglas,
Isle of Man,
British Isles.

While every effort is made to keep prices low, it is sometimes necessary to increase prices at short notice. Star Books reserve the right to show new retail prices on covers which may differ from those advertised in the text or elsewhere.

Postage and Packing Rate
UK: 45p for the first book, 20p for the second book and 14p for each additional book ordered to a maximum charge of £1.63. BFPO and EIRE: 45p for the first book, 20p for the second book, 14p per copy for the next 7 books thereafter 8p per book. Overseas: 75p for the first book and 21p per copy for each additional book.